MR. CHICKEE'S FUNNY MONEY

MR. CHICKEE'S
FUNNY MONEY

CHRISTOPHER PAUL CURTIS

WENDY
LAMB
BOOKS

Published by
Wendy Lamb Books
an imprint of
Random House Children's Books
a division of Random House, Inc.
New York

Visit us on the Web! www.randomhouse.com/kids
Educators and librarians, for a variety of teaching tools, visit us at
www.randomhouse.com/teachers

Library of Congress Cataloging-in-Publication Data is available upon request.

ISBN: 0-385-32772-2 (trade)
       0-385-90936-5 (lib. bdg.)

Printed in the United States of America

October 2005

10 9 8 7 6 5 4 3 2 1

BVG

To Steven, Cydney, and Hara

ONE

A Bad Ending to a Good Summer

STEVEN SAT ON THE BANKS of the Flint River below the Kearsley Dam crying. Not just little splishy-splashy tears either—his tears were gooshy waterfalls coming out of his eyes. He was crying so hard that the tears weren't just running down his cheeks, they were running over his forehead into his hair and sideways into his ears!

But who could blame him? Even though he was nine and one-third years old and probably a genius he was boo-hooing like a kindergarten baby because he'd just seen the most horrible thing any kid could ever see. Well, almost.

His best friend for this week, his greatest pal ever, the only one he'd ever shared all his secrets with, was gone. Not gone for the weekend or to a new neighborhood or to a new town or even out of the country. He was gone forever!

Steven kept his eyes on the churning and boiling and splashing water at the base of the dam, but deep down inside him he knew. No one, no matter how big and strong they were, could fall over that dam and hold their breath for fifteen minutes, and that was how long it had been.

Gone. That one word kept coming into Steven's mind. It stopped that other word, that other four-letter word. He didn't want to think of both that *other* four-letter word that began and ended with *d* and his best friend in the same sentence.

For the first few minutes after he'd dragged himself out of the water Steven had stared at the spot where they had landed. He kept saying, "Come on! Come on, where are you?"

He'd always believed that if you thought about something hard enough and positively enough you could make it happen, so for ten minutes he kept imagining his friend popping to the surface of the water, gasping and gulping in huge lungfuls of precious air before finally swimming over to the riverbank, where Steven would help pull him out.

After he had imagined this over and over and over and after no head came to the surface, Steven knew, he knew he'd been very lucky in the two-hundred-and-fifty-foot fall over the dam. His friend had not.

Steven sat on the riverbank in shock. A pretty good-sized puddle that mixed Flint River water and tears was growing around him but he didn't care, he didn't even put his face in his hands, he just stuck his face out and cried.

Crashing down the bank toward him through a jungle of thrown-out refrigerators and TVs and plastic garbage bags and weeds were six men all dressed in black suits with white shirts and red neckties. One of them yelled, "Over here! The little boy's alive! He's down here!"

All six men held objects that looked like teeny-weeny satellite dishes. All six dishes were going "Beep! Beep! Beep!" and flashing green and blue lights. The man who had spotted Steven pointed his dish and it beeped faster and faster as he got nearer.

Steven didn't even care. His friend had only been gone for a few minutes and already Steven felt so bad and lonely and sad that nothing seemed important.

The man crouched beside him and said, "There, there, son, it's going to be all right."

Steven felt like he was dreaming when the man took off his black suit jacket and wrapped it around his shoulders. "I'll call an ambulance. You've got a pretty nasty bump on your head there and we don't want to take any chances."

It didn't even seem strange when the man started talking into his watch: "Come in, base, Agent One here, I've got an injury at the bottom of the dam. Subject A Three has suffered a possible concussion and appears to be disoriented, request an ambulance at"—the man looked at his little satellite dish—"at coordinates nine oh three tristar three eight seven ooga-booga three three three four. Over."

The watch answered the man, "One, is A Three in possession of the item? Does he still have it?"

Agent One pointed his mini-dish at Steven. It went "Beep! Beep! Beep!"

One answered, "I'm afraid not, base, that's a negative."

The watch said, "Oh, no, this is terrible, he must've lost it in the fall over the dam. Is A Three alert enough to be questioned?"

Agent One gently shook Steven and said, "Son? Son, are you okay?"

What kind of question was that? How could someone be okay when they knew their best friend was de . . . was gone? Steven just looked at the man.

"Now, son," Agent One said, "you've got to help us out here. Things will be a lot easier if you cooperate, all right?"

Steven nodded, not because he agreed, but because he knew that was what the man wanted him to do.

"Okay, good boy. Now, where is it? We're pretty sure you had it when you two started running across the top of the dam. Did you drop it in the water? Do you know which side it fell on? Just tell me where it is and maybe I can help you out and you won't have to go to jail for too long."

Steven had to think about this. He wished his head would stop spinning for a second so he could make the kind of decision a good detective would about what he should do next.

One thing he did know, spinning head or not, was that this man didn't really care about helping him. He was trying to scare him with that talk about jail, and it worked—Steven started wondering what bad thing could happen next.

"Look, kid, tell me where it is or things could get pretty bad for you." The man's tone changed.

"He . . . he . . . he . . ." Steven pointed at the spot where they'd landed in the water. "He must still have it. I think he swallowed it while we were falling."

One aimed his mini-dish at the spot where Steven pointed. The dish went "Ba-weep! Ba-weep! Ba-weep!"

One yelled into his watch, "Base, base! Subject B One allegedly still has the item in his possession! I'm getting a positive reading on my parabolic unit indicating the item is underwater at the foot of the dam!"

Steven knew what that meant and started getting dizzy all over again.

He put his hand on his forehead and felt a lump the size of a Ping-Pong ball. It was then that that other four-letter word finally came to him. He knew he had to say it.

"Dead," Steven mumbled. "He's dead."

The agent said, "Well, if he isn't he's doing a pretty good imitation of it."

Steven sat down, so shook up that he felt like he was half passed out, half passed in.

The five other men in black suits found him and Agent One and talked into their watches while they pointed their mini-dishes at the water.

". . . yes, sir, Agent Fondoo, we've almost got it . . ."

". . . negative, base, no sign other than parabolic indication . . ."

". . . that's correct . . ."

". . . Ba-weep! Ba-weep! Ba-weep . . ."

5

"... ambulance en route for the little pain in the neck ..."

"... city officials have been contacted ..."

"... affirmative ..."

"... dam will be shut off in twelve hours ..."

"... body of B One and the item will be recovered ..."

"... Ba-weep! Ba-weep! Ba-weep ..."

Steven's head spun and spun but he kept asking himself how this had happened. How had this terrible nightmare started?

It started with Mr. Othello Chickee, a good friend who had given Steven a very strange gift.

As he heard the scream of a siren coming nearer and nearer Steven forced himself to remember it all. He searched his mind to see if he could've stopped this from happening or done something different and changed this horrible ending to his summer, with his best friend tangled up in the weeds at the bottom of a dam and him about to go to prison.

As the men put Steven on a stretcher and started pulling him up the riverbank he remembered exactly how this nightmare had started. . . .

TWO

Mr. Chickee's Gift

STEVEN KNEW THAT MR. CHICKEE liked him better than the rest of the kids in the neighborhood. It wasn't just that Steven's dad and Mr. Chickee were friends either: Mr. Chickee knew everybody and was friends with all the adults on Flint's south side. But of all the boys around eight or nine or ten years old, Steven was the only one who always gave Mr. Chickee the proper respect and didn't treat him like there was something wrong with him. Steven looked at Mr. Chickee with an open mind, which is the way a detective has to look at everything.

When the other kids would tell fantastic stories and tall tales about Mr. Chickee and his being blind, Steven would twist up his face and try to ignore them or try to set them straight.

Andre Warrington had said that Mr. Chickee wasn't blind at all, that he was really a secret agent hired by the government to spy on people in the neighborhood.

"If that's true," Steven had said, "where does he keep his badge, his gun and his walkie-talkie? Have you ever seen a secret agent without those?"

That was enough to make Andre Warrington quit talking nonsense.

Smudge Munday had said that his mother had told him that Mr. Chickee used to be a jet fighter pilot during the Civil War and that he'd gone blind when he flew too close to the sun while chasing a UFO and took his sunglasses off to get a better look.

Steven had shut Smudge up too when he asked, "If that's true, how did he land his plane without blowing it up and killing himself? And if he was blind why didn't the aliens beam themselves onto his plane and steal all the top-secret information?"

Smudge had given Steven a look that went from being confused to being dirty.

Daniel Love had said that Mr. Chickee's white cane had supersecret sneaky scientific stuff in it that warned Mr. Chickee when a car was coming or who was walking toward him or where a telephone pole was.

Steven had said, "If that's true, where are the batteries or the extension cord to run the scientific stuff, and where's the warning buzzer?"

This had left Daniel Love scratching his head.

Stevie Boy Collins had said that he'd dreamed that Mr. Chickee was actually a person from another world called Ourside who had come to Earth and had designed a series of tests to find a lost genius who was his civilization's one hope to translate a mysterious message that was the only thing that could save them from certain destruction and death.

But that was so bizarre that Steven hadn't needed to say anything—they'd all ignored Stevie Boy.

The kids knew that Steven used to have a subscription to the magazine *Young Detectives' Journal* and it was well known that he was the second-smartest student at Clark Elementary School, just behind Richelle Cyrus-Herndon, so they figured he was probably right.

Smudge Munday still wasn't buying it. "Okay, Mr. Know-It-All," Smudge said, "how does he know when to cross the street or how not to bump into stuff?"

Steven was ready for this question since he'd asked his dad the same thing a long time ago.

"Easy, he's got the whole south side rememorized, he's lived here for almost a hundred years and he taps with his cane to make sure nothing's in his way."

Steven's dad had actually said that Mr. Chickee had been living in the neighborhood for almost thirty-five years but Steven knew that a little exaggerating always makes a fact sound better.

Smudge and Andre and Daniel and Stevie Boy had to agree that Steven's answers made more sense than spacemen, magic canes, spies and mysterious messages. But they

9

still ran behind Mr. Chickee acting silly or spoke to him and then made goofy faces.

So it was easy to see why Steven was Mr. Chickee's favorite boy in the neighborhood. Mr. Chickee might've been blind, but that didn't mean he couldn't see what was going on.

Mr. Chickee was Steven's favorite adult too. He helped relieve the Saturday-morning boredom that he felt after he'd watched the hour of cartoons Mom and Dad allowed, and after the meeting of the Flint Future Detectives Club was over.

Every Saturday morning at around 8:05 Steven would make sure he was playing near the corner of Liberty Street and the alley. When he'd hear the tap-tap-tap of a cane coming near, he'd stop whatever he was doing and run over to Mr. Chickee.

"Well, young fellow," Mr. Chickee would say before Steven could say a word, "how's life treating you?"

"Fine, Mr. Chickee, how's life treating you?"

"Oh," Mr. Chickee would say every Saturday morning at around 8:05 and fifteen seconds, "not bad for such an old fart."

And every Saturday morning Steven laughed at the same old joke.

"You going to get groceries, Mr. Chickee?"

"Sure am, can you give me a hand today?"

"Uh-huh, I already told Mom."

"Good, good, you wanna carry my cart?"

Steven always got to pull the small two-wheeled wire basket for Mr. Chickee's groceries. They walked together to Mitchell's Food Fair, spent their usual hour or so shopping and started home.

At around 9:07 when they hit Liberty Street and the alley Mr. Chickee said the same thing every Saturday: "Well, Steven, I don't understand it, two handsome devils like you and me walked eight blocks together and no women attacked us! I tell you, these Flint women are something else. If we were back in Philly it'd be a whole different story."

And just like he did every Saturday around 9:07 and twenty-two seconds, Steven said, "You probably didn't hear them, Mr. Chickee, but there have been nine or ten of the finest women in the world following us for the last three blocks. But they all look kind of shy."

Mr. Chickee said, "You know, I think I heard something on the radio about there being a meeting of something called the World's Finest, Most Shy Women Club going on here in Flint this weekend, so I guess that explains it, huh? We'd better separate here and hurry on home before they get their nerve up and jump us. As usual you were a gentleman and . . ."

Just like every other Saturday, Steven finished the sentence, ". . . and a scholar . . ."

And Mr. Chickee said, ". . . and most importantly an inspiration to be with, thank you very much, young Mr. Carter."

"You're welcome, Mr. Chickee."

11

But on this Saturday, something different happened. Mr. Chickee took the small cart from Steven and started down Liberty Street. Before he'd tapped four times he called, "You think I've forgotten something, don't you?"

"Yes!" Steven thought.

Usually while they were in Mitchell's Food Fair Mr. Chickee would have Steven pick up a big bottle of Vernor's ginger ale and a bag of Paramount potato chips for himself, but today he hadn't.

Steven had been kind of surprised but he didn't mind, he didn't spend Saturday mornings with Mr. Chickee to get a reward, he did it because it made him feel important and helpful to tell what was on sale and what looked fresh and what looked nasty.

But he would kind of miss his Saturday ginger ale and potato chips.

"I haven't forgotten at all," Mr. Chickee said. "You see, Steven, I'm going back to Philly this afternoon for a couple of months and before I left I wanted to give you a special thanks for always being so helpful and so cheerful. I always look forward to my Saturdays with Steven."

Mr. Chickee reached in his jacket pocket and handed an envelope to Steven. "I've had this for quite a while now and it's time for me to pass it on. I've always known you're the person who'd know what to do with it."

Steven held the envelope up to the sky and could see the outline of a green rectangular paper in it, sort of like a dollar bill.

"Thank you, Mr. Chickee, but my parents said I'm not allowed to take money from anyone."

Mr. Chickee laughed and said, "Steven, I insist. But don't open it until later. Remember this: It's not what you think it is. I know you'll carefully reason out what's best to be done with it."

Steven had tried to follow his folks' rule but Mr. Chickee *had* insisted, so what was a kid to do? Maybe Mr. Chickee wanted Steven to buy two months' worth of chips and Vernor's while he was gone to Philadelphia.

"Well, okay, Mr. Chickee, thank you very much. See you in a couple of months! I'll miss my Saturdays with Mr. Othello Chickee."

Mr. Chickee smiled, turned and tap-tap-tapped toward his home. As he made his way down Liberty Street people called from their porches and yards, "Hello, Mr. Chickee!"

"Morning, Margaret."

"Beautiful day, Othello!"

"It sure is, Wes!"

"My man, Othello, what's up?"

"Nothing but the rent, Theodore!"

"Good morning, Mr. Chickee!"

"How do, Miss Davidson?"

Steven stuffed the envelope into his back pocket and ran to the oak tree behind the Riddles' house where he spent his Saturday afternoons reading comic books, chugging down Vernor's and munching potato chips. He climbed up to his favorite branch and pulled out Mr. Chickee's gift.

"Remember this," Mr. Chickee had said, "it's not what you think it is."

"Hmmm," Steven said to himself, "I think it's a dollar bill, so if it's not what I think then what else could it be?"

He held the envelope up to the sky again. The shape and color of what was inside seemed to perfectly match a dollar.

"Maybe if it's not a dollar it's a five! Or maybe it's a ten! Or"—Steven took a big breath—"maybe it's a one-hundred-dollar bill!"

He couldn't help himself, he ripped the envelope open.

It was money, all right, but he couldn't tell how much it was worth from the side he was looking at. There was only a picture of an old building and words around the picture saying "Seal of the United States Department of Treasury."

"Huh?" he said, and flipped it over to the front. There in the center of the bill was a drawing of the head of a very serious-looking man.

Mr. Chickee had said he should carefully reason about what to do with it.

"Hmmm," Steven said. He'd noticed how on TV and in the movies, anytime a really smart person was about to say something they always said "Hmmm" first. "Judging by the look on this guy's face he either just got punched in the stomach or he's just getting ready to rip a really big fart."

In the upper left- and lower right-hand corners of the bill were bunches and bunches of zeroes following a number one.

Steven counted the zeroes in the corner: ". . . twelve, thirteen, fourteen, fifteen. Fifteen zeroes? A one and fifteen zeroes? Is Mr. Chickee playing some kind of joke on me?"

He thought a bit more like a detective and decided careful reasoning didn't have a whole lot to do with either getting gut-punched or passing large amounts of gas. So he looked a little harder at the unsmiling face on the bill.

The man was very unhappy-looking, very sweaty and covered with lots and lots of hair. Under his picture where the dead president's name was usually written were the letters *HWMISB*.

Steven tried to pronounce this word but his mouth couldn't get around all the consonants. It didn't seem like there were enough vowels in there.

Since he was the founder, president, chief executive officer and secretary of the Flint Future Detectives Club he knew he was stumped, and that was when a detective had to do lots of research and talk to the experts to help explain the mystery.

"Oh, no," Steven said, climbing down the tree, "I don't really know any experts, so I guess I have to talk to the only people I know who *think* they know everything. I'll have to ask Mom and Dad about Mr. Chickee's funny money."

THREE

Getting Closer to the Truth

"DAD, WHAT IS A ONE with fifteen zeroes after it?"

Even though this was an honest question Steven was being kind of sneaky. This was also a test for Dad, and Steven was betting that his father was going to fail.

If Dad did manage to pass this first question Steven planned to ask him a couple more, and if, by some miracle, Dad passed those then he'd get a reward. But the odds were that it would never get that far. Steven had a pretty good idea what Dad's reaction would be and sure enough, Dad didn't let him down.

Dad lowered the newspaper he was reading into his lap and as he spoke, Steven silently said each word to himself a second before it passed his father's lips. He would've moved his lips right along with Dad but Steven knew that that qualified as sass and not a whole lot of that was tolerated.

"Steven," Dad sighed, "what grade are you in now?"

"Fourth."

"Fourth," Dad repeated. "Well, that's plenty old enough and you're plenty smart enough to get the dictionary and look it up."

"But look what up?"

"What do you think a one with fifteen zeroes is?"

"I don't know, a jillion?"

"Look it up."

"Is it a zillion?"

"Look it up."

"A skillion?"

"Get your great-great-grandfather's dictionary down and look all three of those words up."

One of the things Steven hated most was using Great-great-grampa Carter's dictionary. He felt like there was something about the old book that just wasn't right.

The book seemed to have a really bad attitude.

Once Steven had tried to figure out just how old it was. He'd turned to the copyright page at the front and instead of seeing a date he read, "You're not a librarian, what are you doing on this page?"

Later he went back to see if he'd read it right. This time instead of a date it read, "You again! Get a life and leave me alone."

He knew he had to tell somebody about this. If he'd told his father that the dictionary was telling him things, Dad would only have said something like "Oh, really. I hope it's telling you to pay closer attention in your math class."

17

But Mom was different, so he'd told her, "Mom! That old dictionary is talking to me!"

She'd said, "Steven! That's wonderful! I know exactly how you feel—when I was a little girl I used to think books were alive too! Maybe not the dictionary, but books like M. C. *Higgins, the Great* and *To Kill a Mockingbird* really seemed to be talking to *me*."

Steven said, "No, Mom, it can't really talk, it's a book! It's leaving me messages and it's not very friendly!"

When Mom and Steven checked the copyright page again there was nothing but some faded dates.

Mom had given Steven a sad look and said, "Maybe you shouldn't be reading this dictionary, Steven. I think I'll have a talk with your father about that."

That sounded like some good advice and Steven hadn't gone back to the dictionary for a long time. But now Dad had ordered him to so he didn't have any choice.

He got the step stool out and reached up on the highest shelf to pull the old dictionary down.

"Man!" he said. "It's getting heavier all the time."

He turned to the copyright page to see if maybe another message was waiting for him there.

He read, "Of course I'm getting heavier, language is something that never stops growing so I'm adding new words all the time. Words you probably know very well, like a couple that seem to come to mind when you're near, *diminutive* and *dunce*. (*Diminutive*. *[di-MIN-ya-tiv] adj. Small, little, tiny. Dunce [dunts] n. A dull-witted, ignorant person. [1520–1530] After John Duns Scotus, whose writings were attacked by the humanists as foolish.)"*

Steven frowned and the dictionary wrote, "Don't take it personally, but I call 'em like I see 'em!"

Steven slammed the book shut.

"Okay, I came here to look up words, not get disrespected by some book."

He looked up *skillion* first, then *jillion* and *zillion* and reported back to his father.

"It says a jillion and a zillion are large, inexact numbers, it doesn't say anything about a skillion."

Dad was way too predictable.

"All right," he said, "bring me a pencil and a piece of paper. Let's see if we can't figure this out."

Steven already had them in his hand. Dad gave him a strange look.

"Okay," Dad said, and on the left side of the paper he wrote a one and three zeroes, "what number is this?"

"A thousand."

"Uh-huh." Dad added three more zeroes. "And this?"

Steven counted the six zeroes. "A million."

"Exactly."

Steven had known all this was coming and had thought of writing a one with three, then six, then nine, then twelve, then fifteen zeroes before he handed the paper to Dad but that was getting a little too close to sass again. Besides, it wasn't always a good idea to let your parents know you knew what they were thinking. Sometimes it was best if they kept believing you were just a silly kid instead of a very wise soon-to-be-top-notch detective and the second-smartest kid at Clark Elementary School.

"Okay, Steven." Three more zeroes were added. "This is a . . . ?"

"A billion?"

"Are you asking me or telling me?"

"Telling you?"

"Very good, and when we add three more?"

Now it was getting tough. Steven's experience with really big, gigantic, humongous numbers actually only went up to 635,541.

On the first day of second grade Steven had asked Miss Henry how big a million was. Miss Henry was a new teacher and thought Steven's question was wonderful so she started a project. She decided to have her students collect as many soda pop bottle tops as they could so they would see that a million was an easy number to say but a very difficult number to reach.

Poor Miss Henry didn't realize how smart and hardworking and enthusiastic they were so she was quite shocked when by March seventeenth they had collected 635,541 tops. This wasn't quite enough to make a million, but it was just enough to cause the collapse of the closet floor where they were being stored. When the floor gave way all the tops fell into the empty kindergarten room directly below.

Stevie Boy Collins was in the principal's office, as usual, when Miss Henry was called in to explain.

During recess he imitated Mrs. Ricks saying to Miss Henry, "Suzanne, you failed to show your students what a million soda pop bottle tops would look like, but the janitor has assured me that the collapse of my closet floor into the kindergarten room has caused the death of at least two and a half million cockroaches. These disgusting, unfortunate insects have apparently been using your project as an incubator for the past six months.

"Don't grieve too long, though, the janitor tells me another three million of the reprehensible vermin have survived this disaster and have taken up residence elsewhere in my school. I am assuming you will not mind paying for the exterminator out of your salary, hmmm?"

Stevie Boy's imitation of Mrs. Ricks scolding Miss Henry got to be famous throughout the school and caused him to have another meeting of his own with the principal.

Now, as Steven stared at Dad's one with twelve zeroes he was in a land way beyond 635,541. He was in Guess Land.

"Well?" Dad said.

"A trillion?"

Dad smiled. "Excellent. Now for the top prize, can my little knuckleheaded son put a name on a one with fifteen zeroes after it?" Dad added another three zeroes. "What is this number?"

"I don't know, Dad, I . . ." Uh-oh, a whiny tone was coming into Steven's voice.

"Think—what is the pattern in the words given to the numbers? Lots of times words have patterns and if you can figure out the pattern you can figure out what comes next. Think!"

Steven hated questions like this. Usually they made his brain shut right down. But this time he decided, "If Dad puts me through one of these stupid quizzes I'm not going to share Mr. Chickee's funny money with him when I cash it in."

"Think!" Thunk. Dad's finger thunked Steven's forehead.

Steven said, "Uh . . ."

"Think!" Thunk!

"Uh . . ."

"Just look at the pattern. What does *bi* mean?"

"To get something from the store?"

"Not spelled *b-u-y*, spelled *b-i*, as in *bicycle*."

Steven's brain unlocked. "Oh! It means two."

"Right. And what does *tri*, as in *tricycle*, mean?"

"Three."

"Hey, hey, hey! So what's next? We've got billion, trillion, then what? What's next in the pattern? What is the prefix meaning four?"

Steven could feel his brain shutting down again.

"Uh, let's see, is it a fourillion?"

The way Dad's eyebrows jammed together told Steven this was a real bad guess.

"Fourillion?" Dad asked. "Have you ever heard of a fourillion?"

"Well, I—"

22

"No, you haven't. What would you call four babies born at the same time to the same mother?"

Steven almost said, "I'd call them Andre, Monte, Shonte, and Ronde," but before he could open his mouth the sass-warning light went on and he said, "They'd be quadruplets."

"Exactly. And you've studied enough biology to know what an animal that walks on four legs is called."

This was starting to make sense. "It's a quadruped."

"Very good! That's my boy, now you're doing it, now you're thinking!"

"Yeah," Steven said to himself, "I'm thinking that all your teasing has cost you a whole lot of money this time, funny guy."

"Now for the biggie. What is the next number in this sequence: million, billion, trillion . . ."

Steven shouted, "Quaddillion!"

"Quadrillion," Dad corrected him.

"Oh."

"Look it up, Steven."

Steven got his small pocket dictionary out. It didn't have any attitude at all. He found: "Quadrillion. Noun. The cardinal number equal to ten to the fifteenth power." Finally! The piece of money folded in his pocket had a proper name—it was a quadrillion-dollar bill. That much of the mystery was solved.

He really hesitated about asking the next question.

"Oh, well," he thought, "better get this over with before

I get my hopes up too high and start thinking I'm a quadrillionaire."

Dad had gone back to reading his newspaper.

"Dad?"

"Hmmm?"

"What is the biggest piece of money there is?"

"Uh, let me think . . ." Dad put the paper in his lap and started rubbing his chin. This was a sign that he was about to go off the deep end silly-wise.

"I remember now, I believe it's in Papua New Guinea. They used large stones for money and I seem to recall that the biggest one was a four-ton two-dollar bill owned by the Rama-dama-ding-dong family."

"Dad, you know what I mean."

"Frame the question properly, please."

Steven let air come out of his mouth in a long puff. He didn't want to go back and take any stuff from that old dictionary again.

"Okay," he said, "what is the largest . . . oh, boy, what is the largest . . . decombination . . ."

"Denomination."

"What is the largest-denomination bill in U.S. currentry?"

"*Cee,*" Dad said, "U.S. curren-*cy.*"

With Dad's nonstop tutoring Steven was afraid he'd be a lawyer before he turned twelve years old. Or even worse, an English teacher.

"Okay," Dad said, "I think that the thousand-dollar bill is the largest bill in public circulation, but I believe there might be one-hundred-thousand-dollar bills that go from bank to bank."

"One hundred thousand dollars is all?"

"I think so. Why do you sound so disappointed?"

"No reason." Steven wasn't about to give up this easily. "So that would mean that anything larger than one hundred thousand dollars is fake?"

"No," Dad said, and Steven's dying hopes flickered back to life, "not fake, it would be real. Real counterfeit cash."

"Ha ha," Steven said. He knew that meant fake money.

Dad said, "Wait, let me guess what all these questions are about. I'll bet you and your pal Russell found a quadrillion-dollar bill and Mr. Mitchell didn't have quite enough change on hand to cash it so you guys had to put your candy and comic books back, right?" Dad's nose went back into his newspaper.

"Dad . . ."

"Bye-bye, Steven."

"Bye."

"Yeah," Steven thought as he walked to the front door, "bye-bye to any chance you'll ever have of helping me spend this cash." He laughed as he walked outside. Yup, old know-it-all Dad had really blown it by not being more serious with Steven's important questions. Sure, Steven would probably end up giving Dad a couple of billion dollars once he'd cashed Mr. Chickee's funny money, but the really big bucks would be under the control of Mr. Steven Daemon Carter.

And maybe Mom.

25

And maybe, maybe Russell.

But Steven's mind was locked—old smart-answer-can't-stop-teasing Dad was going to be frozen out with only a billion or two, and not a penny more.

Maybe then Dad would learn the proper way to answer the questions of a very serious future detective.

FOUR

Russell and Zoopy

"HEYA, BUCKO!" IT WAS Russell Woods. Russell had the habit of calling everyone Bucko, but he seemed to get a really big kick out of using this name on Steven.

"Heya, Russ."

"Well, what did your mom and dad say about Mr. Chickee's funny money? Are we rich?"

"I didn't tell them I had it."

"Why not, Bucko? I wanna buy that bike and I don't mean maybe."

Russell was seven years old but sometimes he acted like he was three. When he acted kid-ish it seemed worse than it was because Russell was so doggone big. Even though he was two years younger than Steven he was four inches taller and fifty pounds heavier! Like Steven's father had said, "That Russell Woods is one real hunk of a kid!"

The way he acted, Russell reminded Steven of the Woodses' pet, Zoopy.

Two years before, the day Russell's family moved in next door, Steven's eyes had almost popped out of his head when he looked into the back of their minivan.

There was the biggest, furriest, roundest black and brown animal filling up the whole inside of the van and from where Steven sat on his porch watching he thought his new neighbors must own the world's shortest, fattest pony or the world's largest guinea pig.

When Steven walked over to the van for a better look, the animal turned around and gave a giant *"Ah-oof!"*

The sound was so loud that the van shook and before he knew what he was doing Steven jumped back four feet.

When his heart quieted down he heard a laugh behind him. A boy was standing there with his hand over his mouth. He was ten or eleven years old.

"He won't bite," the boy giggled, "he's just Zoopy! See?"

He pointed at the van and the animal licked the window. It looked like someone was scrubbing the window with a giant pink towel.

"Yuck, Zoopy!" the boy said. He pulled the side door open and the van wobbled back and forth when the animal jumped out.

It had to be the biggest dog in the world!

The dog bounded over to the boy and, with a sound like

water running out of a bathtub, he licked the kid's face. When the dog's tongue went back in his mouth the boy looked like he'd just jumped out of a swimming pool.

Steven started to laugh but stopped when the kid took a deep breath, put his fists over his eyes and yelled, "Mummy!" Giant tears splashed from him and mixed with the dog's kiss.

"Wow!" Steven thought. "This guy's a big baby. I haven't cried like that in about a billion years." (Actually it had been six weeks.)

The dog tilted his head and raised his ears as the boy kept screaming. Steven walked over and put his hand on the kid's shoulder. "Hey, don't cry, I don't think he meant to get you all wet, that's probably the only way he knows how to say hi."

"He does it all the time and I hate it. I wish he'd quit!"

The tears slowed down. Steven knew that a joke at a time like this always helped.

"Well," he said, "you know what I'd do? To get even with Zoopy I'd run right up to him and lick him back!"

The boy's eyes grew. "You would?" A smile came to his wet face.

"Yup," Steven said, "that would show him!"

Steven felt really good because the boy began laughing. This kid acted very strange, he seemed more like a kinder-gartner than a fifth or sixth grader.

The boy ran at the dog with his tongue aimed like a lit-tle pink arrow. Just as the kid reached him Zoopy's tongue came out and the boy's head disappeared in the sloppy wet pink towel for a second time.

Steven couldn't help laughing. The boy laughed too. And just as it happens so many times, that good shared laugh was the sound of a great friendship being born.

"So," Steven asked, "how's he taste?"

"Not too bad, but it seems like they used too much salt when they made him."

They both laughed until their stomachs hurt. Finally Steven asked his new friend his name.

"I'm Russell Braithewaite Woods."

"How old are you, Russell?"

Russell spread all the fingers on his right hand and held them up.

"*Five?*" Steven yelled.

"Uh-huh," the boy said. "Mummy and Daddy are making me start kindergarten at Clark Elementary School as soon as summer is gone. But I'm gonna do a lot of crying to get them to change their mind."

"But you're so big! No one at the school is as big as you!"

"No one? Not even the teachers? Not even the custodians?"

"Well, you're bigger than Mrs. Bracy, but she's mean."

"How mean? Does she yell at kids?"

"Sure, but don't worry, she teaches sixth grade. You won't have to be in her class for a long time."

"Whew, I don't like mean people, even if they are littler than me."

"You'll be the biggest kid at Clark and this is the biggest dog in the world. How old is he?"

"He's this much." Russell held up one finger and bent it toward his palm.

"How much is that?"

"Half."

"Half a year? This dog is only six months old?"

"Uh-huh."

"Wow! What kind of dog is he?"

"I don't know, he's regular."

"Is he part Saint Bernard?"

"My daddy says his mother must've been a hippopotamus and his father was probably a bear. Daddy says if he gets any bigger he's got to hit the road, Jack."

Steven looked at the dog. It *was* as big as a bear but silly-looking too, sort of like Russell.

Steven gave his best look of disgust. "Who named him Zoopy?"

"I did. When we first got him he was this big." Russell put his hand about a foot above the ground. "Then the day after that, *Zoop!* He was this big." Russell raised his hand another foot. "Then the day after that, *Zoop!* He was this big, so I figured it was some kind of magic and thought his name should be Zoopy.

"My dad hates that name, he wanted to call him Simba, that's African talk for lion, but I got a lot of crying in and Dad quit. You probably think my dad was right, huh? You probably think Zoopy's a stupid name too."

Steven looked at the enormous puppy sitting with his tongue out looking like he was waiting to lick somebody again. A bird flew by and the pup noticed it and shut his mouth with a loud clop. His ears perked up and he let out three more tremendous *"Ah-oof!"*s. Both Steven and Russell put their hands over their ears.

The bird disappeared and Zoopy forgot about it and sat there with his tongue dangling out.

"Nope," Steven thought, "this dog is no Simba, this dog is a big, goofy, sweet Zoopy."

He said, "I think you gave him a perfect name, Russell."

Russell laughed. "Yeah, me too. I just wish his tongue wasn't so big and nasty."

Even though Russell and Zoopy were two goofs they became Steven's two best friends that summer.

Now they were the only ones Steven had told about his quadrillion-dollar bill and Russell couldn't wait to spend it. Number one on Russell's list of things to buy was an eighteen-speed mountain bike with flames painted on the side.

". . . huh, Bucko? How much longer? When are you going to ask your folks if our funny money is real?"

"Russ, we've got to wait awhile. If the adults get a hold of it they'll take it away from us. Remember, we're Flint Future Detectives and we've got to investigate all the things that can happen to our quadrillion-dollar bill. Mr. Chickee said we have to do some careful reasoning about this and I'm gonna do it."

"Okay, Bucko, but let's hurry up so we can start spending. How long do you think this investigating and reasoning stuff is going to take?"

In some ways Russell was right. Steven had had the quadrillion-dollar bill for two days now and he still didn't know too much more about it than when Mr. Chickee had given it to him. Maybe it was time to quit pretending he was investigating and reasoning and actually show the bill to Mom and Dad.

"Okay, Russell, I'll go figure out the evidence to see if we should tell my parents or if we should wait to show it to someone else, deal?"

"Deal. But don't get mad if your dad acts like he doesn't care too much about our money. When I told Mummy and Daddy about it they just smiled and said, 'That's nice, boy, go in the backyard and play and don't spend that money all in one place.'"

"Aww, Russell! You promised not to say anything about it! Why'd you tell them?"

"Oops," Russell said, "I don't know, Bucko, I guess I forgot."

Steven couldn't really complain. "I don't know" and "I forgot" used to be his two favorite things to say to Mom and Dad. He'd said them so many times that Dad had banned him from ever saying them again until he was twenty-one years old.

But that wasn't all Dad had done. He made two rules, one that if Steven was going to answer one of his parents'

33

questions with "I don't know," he had to put his left thumb on his nose and wiggle his ears three times. If the answer to something Mom and Dad asked was "I forgot," he had to say "ChakaKhan, ChakaKhan, ChakaKhan" in a real deep voice and stick his tongue out as far as it would go.

Dad thought this would embarrass Steven so much that he'd never want to not know something or forget anything ever again. But after three weeks of doing this Steven could speak this new language like a pro.

There were problems with it, though. One was that Steven started doing it without even knowing he was doing it.

At school Mr. Punga had said, "Steven Carter, why didn't you do your math homework?"

Steven said, "Sorry, Mr. Punga . . ." Then he went "ChakaKhan, ChakaKhan, ChakaKhan," in a real deep voice and stuck his tongue out at his teacher.

That was the first time Steven had to go visit the principal's office.

Another problem with this silly language was when Dad asked him too many hard questions in a row, like: "Steven?"

"Yes, Dad?"

"Where are all your white socks? Didn't I tell you to get them into the wash?"

Thumb on nose, ears wiggle, wiggle, wiggle.

"What do you mean you don't know? Didn't I tell you not to throw them around and to get them in the dirty clothes?"

34

"Yes, Dad, but . . . ChakaKhan, ChakaKhan, ChakaKhan," tongue out.

"How could you forget? Where did you put them after you took them off?"

Thumb on nose, ears wiggle, wiggle, wiggle.

"How can you possibly not know?"

"ChakaKhan, ChakaKhan, ChakaKhan," tongue out.

"Well, why don't you start a little search party and round up all those socks? Then how about a two-page essay titled something like, oh, I don't know, how about something like 'How to Be More Responsible'?"

"Aww, man, Dad, that's not fair, I didn't do it on purpose, it's just that sometimes I get so busy I just ChakaKhan, ChakaKhan, ChakaKhan," tongue out.

"Some of the time I don't know about you, Steven."

"Man," Steven thought, "if he thinks I say the same things over and over he should listen to himself once in a while. How many millions of times have I heard him say 'Some of the time I don't know about you, Steven' or 'Steven, you scare me, where on earth do you go?' Or even worse, when he taps me on the head and says 'Hello? Anybody home?'

"Boy, if I was an adult or had a little bit of power," Steven thought, "I'd pay him back, I'd ban *him* from saying those words.

"Whenever he wanted to say 'Some of the time I don't know about you' I'd make him hop in a circle on one foot saying 'Toop, toop, toop,' every time he landed." Even kindergartners knew what *toop* was spelled backward. How embarrassing would that be?

Not everything was bad about talking this way, though. Saying "I forgot" and "I don't know" with gestures had made Steven develop some new muscles and had given him some strange powers.

On his eighth birthday, when the cake was set down in front of him, the lights were dimmed and the candles were lit, Mom said, "Okay, birthday boy, blow 'em out." Steven said "I don't know" in Dad's sign language real, real fast about a jillion times. His ears started flapping back and forth so much that a good breeze made the candles on the cake flicker and dance before some of them actually went out!

Steven had only gotten six of them so to get the other two he said in Dad's language "I forgot" so that his tongue zipped out of his mouth four feet and he actually licked the last two candles out!

(Here's a word of warning: NEVER, EVER, EVER LICK THE CANDLES ON A BIRTHDAY CAKE. Steven's tongue hurt for three weeks after this little stunt.)

When Steven's tongue shot out of his mouth like a lizard's it was more than enough for Russell's mom. She snatched Russell from the table and pulled him out the front door mumbling, "I always knew there was something wrong with those Carters! The entire family is possessed by Satan, Lord have mercy on their souls."

So it was easy to see why Steven was sympathetic when

Russell said "I forgot" and "I don't know." Russell's parents hadn't believed a word about the quadrillion-dollar bill anyway so no harm had been done.

". . . huh, Bucko? Are you gonna be mad at me now?"

Steven realized that Russell was asking him another question. "Man," Steven thought, "maybe I do drift away some of the time, but that's okay, when you're a future detective that's called being absentminded."

"Huh, Bucko?"

"Uh, no, Russ, I'm not mad, honest. I'm just trying to figure out how to show this money to Dad without him ignoring it."

"Well, okay . . ."

"All right, Russ, I'll see you later."

"Bucko? Sorry I blabbed. But I'm pretty sure if I hadn't told Mummy and Daddy then Zoopy was going to let them know, so they'd've found out anyway."

Steven laughed. "No problem, Russ, our secret's still safe."

FIVE

The Godfather of What?

THERE WERE THREE PROBLEMS WITH showing Mr. Chickee's funny money to Mom and Dad. Steven dug around in the huge mess on his cluttered desk and found two writing pads. On one he wrote, "Reasons Not to Show Them Mr. Chickee's Gift," and on the second he wrote, "Reasons They Should Get a Look."

Under "Reasons Not to Show Them," he wrote: "#1. Parents might make the quadrillion-dollar bill seem stupid."

Man, was this ever true! With one of her psychology book remarks, like "Oh, Steven! That is so fascinating! I'm so proud that you had both the initiative and the imagination to look further into this," Mom could take the air out of any investigation, and with one roll of his eyes Dad could sink anyone's spirits.

Steven knew the answer to this problem. He wrote, "If parents give discouraging looks or advice that I don't want to hear, just ignore them."

One problem down and three to go.

"#2. If parents think Mr. Chickee's funny money is real they might take it away from me and give me only two or three million dollars."

Steven knew Mom and Dad's intentions might be good and they'd probably say something like "Well, son, let's take it to Mr. So and So and see what he has to say about it." The only problem with that was that they might come home with six or seven new cars and Steven might wake up the next morning living on a yacht or something, and if that happened how could he still be president, chief executive officer and one third of the members of the Flint Future Detectives Club?

To solve this problem Steven wrote, "To make sure they don't snatch my money I have to keep my hands on it at all times."

Two down, one to go.

For "Reasons Not to, #3," he put, "Money can make people act weird."

Steven had seen enough TV and movies and eavesdropped on enough adult conversations to know that money made people do terrible things to each other. There was even that very famous saying, "Money is the roof of all evil," which really didn't make a lot of sense.

For answer #3 he wrote, "If money starts making me act

weird or do crazy things, burn it, bury it, get rid of it, give it away."

Hmmm, three easy solutions. He set that pad aside and began working on the one that said "Reasons They Should Get a Look."

He thought and thought and thought for a good four seconds and could only come up with one: "They're the only ones I trust."

So that was that.

Now came the time to do some hard research, some serious investigating and careful reasoning, and to consult the experts. He walked over to the corner of his room where he kept his official, private, burglar-proof safe.

To anyone who didn't have a highly trained eye Steven's safe might look like a large towel-covered cardboard box that used to hold thirty-six rolls of generic toilet paper. But that was the beauty of it!

If a snoop or a thief or a nosy parent tried to open the box Steven had rigged it so they'd get a snootful of pepper for their trouble!

He carefully undid the boobytrap spring and looked down into his safe. He pushed aside old comic books, broken toys, a couple of supersecret experimental shoes that hadn't worked out very well, stuffed toy dogs, old video games, a flat basketball, loose baseball and basketball cards, dice and the earthly remains of his best friend from three years ago, Harry Hershey, the armless teddy bear. Halfway down in the safe he found what he needed.

The ad in the comic book had called it "The world's only complete three-volume library of the most important information ever gathered on the subjects of private investigating, and reading and controlling strangers' minds, PLUS secret Bokonomist exercises for developing X-ray eyes!" (All at the publisher's clear-out price of $3.98 plus $29.99 shipping and handling!)

Volume one of the library had only eight pages, volume two had six and volume three on X-ray vision was nothing but two pages of a bunch of drawings of eyes looking right and left and up and down and one blank page to be used to practice looking through so you could develop that X-ray vision.

Steven took the seventeen-page stapled-together library to his bed to refresh his memory on private investigating.

Page three of volume one said:

> The most important fact to keep in mind when deciding whether or not to make an arrest or some other important decision is to weigh the evidence. A careful weighing of the evidence is also called for if the true private investigator is about to make any critical life-threatening move.

Right!

He set the two pads of paper next to each other, then carefully lifted them by the corners one at a time. The pad that said "Reasons They Should Get a Look" had twice as many pages in it as the other pad did; therefore, it was heavier. Evidence weighed—case closed.

Mom was still at work and Dad was in the living room reading the newspaper.

Steven didn't know why he was so nervous.

"Oh, well," he thought, "it's now or never."

"Dad?"

"Hmmm?"

Steven hesitated. It was very important to ask this question properly so he could get Dad interested without getting him *too* interested.

"How ya doing?" Steven frowned. This wasn't what he wanted to ask at all.

"Never felt better, never had less." This was another thing Dad said over and over.

"Well, here goes nothing," Steven thought. "Dad, Mr. Chickee gave me some money and I think there's something weird about it."

Dad flipped a couple more pages of the paper.

"Weird, huh?"

"Yeah, it's, uh, strange."

Newspaper pages flipped.

"Be more specific, please. Weird and strange in what way?"

"It's kind of foreign-looking."

"Hmmm. It's not some of that Papua New Guinea money, is it?"

"No, Dad. It looks American but I can't find it online or in any of the encyclopedias or even in Great-great-grampa Carter's crazy dictionary."

Dad flipped more pages of the paper.

"Is it a coin?"

"No, it's paper money."

Dad brought the newspaper down to his lap and looked at Steven.

"Well, what does it say on it? How much is it worth?"

Steven swallowed and whispered, "It's worth a quadrillion dollars!"

"What?"

Steven broke down. "All right, Dad, it's a quadrillion-dollar bill! It's a one with fifteen zeroes after it! Big, big, big, big money!"

Dad brought the newspaper back up.

"Ah, I see. So we're back to that again."

"Yes, Dad, it's just that I—"

"Steven."

"But I just wanted you to tell me if you thought it was real."

"Othello Chickee gave it to you?"

"Yes, Dad."

Dad kept reading. "Then I'm afraid it's not real. Othello hasn't had that kind of money for five or six years."

"Dad, come on, I'm serious."

"Steven?"

"Yes, Dad?"

"I'm not, and neither is a quadrillion-dollar bill."

It was time for some drastic measures. Steven took the cash out of his pocket, pulled the newspaper down and said, "Look!"

Dad squinted and let go of his paper and before Steven could stop him, Dad snatched the money away.

"Hmmm," Dad said before he smiled, "you know, he's looking pretty grim here, but I could swear this is a picture of a young James Brown."

"I knew it!" Steven yelled. "I knew it was real!"

Dad laughed, "Steven, please. This is some sort of very clever advertising gimmick. I'll bet you dollars to doughnuts the back says something like 'You'll save a quadrillion dollars if you shop at Mitchell's Food Fair.' See?"

Dad flipped the bill over and the smile left his face.

"What? The United States Treasury Department in Washington, D.C." Dad flipped the bill over several times. "This *is* strange!"

"See, I told you," Steven yelled, "it's real, isn't it?"

Dad reached into his front pocket and pulled out a ten-dollar bill. He rubbed the ten between his fingers, then did the same thing with the quadrillion-dollar bill.

"I did the same thing with a dollar bill, Dad. They're the same size, the same kind of paper, the same color, the same kind of ink, the same words saying 'This currency is legal tender for all debts public and pri—' "

"Wow!" Dad interrupted, and when he did Steven's heart flew!

"I knew it!" Steven yelled. "I knew it! I'm rich! It's real! Eureka! Geronimo! I'm rich!"

"Steven."

"What am I going to do? What am I going to do?"

Dad said, "The first thing you're going to do is lower your voice and calm down. I didn't say 'wow' because you're rich, I said 'wow' because if Othello is running these off in his basement he's coming real, real, close to counterfeiting. This is obviously a fake."

"A fake?" Steven remembered one of the solutions he'd written on his yellow legal pad. "If parents say anything I don't want to hear—ignore it."

"A fake."

"But, Dad, no one, not even someone as smart as Mr. Chickee, would ever be able to make up something like this. Look at it. It's perfect, it's got to be real!"

Steven could hear his father's mind slamming shut. The newspaper rose again and from behind it Dad said, "Do you know who James Brown is?"

"Yes, Dad. Isn't he that old guy who sued all the rappers because they were using his screams on their CDs and weren't paying him for it? But how much is a scream worth?"

Dad lowered the paper. His forehead wrinkled. Steven wasn't sure if Dad was looking upset because he'd said James Brown's screams weren't worth much or because he'd called James Brown old.

Dad said, "Well, I guess that's partially right, but there's a lot more to James Brown than that."

Steven frowned. This sounded like the beginning of another story about African American musical history. It wasn't that he wasn't interested, it was just that these stories tended to get kind of long and the mystery of Mr. Chickee's funny money needed to be solved right away.

"You see, Steven, James Brown was a very famous, very influential, very innovative entertainer."

"Yup," Steven thought, "another journey into musical roots."

"Most of your great singers and entertainers of today owe more than royalties to James for his screams."

Dad stood up and started pacing—a real bad sign. Steven felt like saying "Just get to the point!" But he knew Dad was on a roll and wouldn't or couldn't stop himself.

"James Brown was the creator of a whole new style of singing, dancing and entertaining. People unconsciously imitate him to this day."

"I wish *I* was unconscious right about now," Steven thought.

"All the little ticky-tacky artists that you listen to today are where they are because James opened so many creative doors for them. He is the original Godfather of Soul. He was truly tremendous.

"About the only thing I didn't like about James was that way back in the late fifties and early sixties . . ." Steven couldn't help groaning out loud. Some of the stories that Dad started in the fifties or sixties ended up back at Noah's ark. ". . . James used to have the biggest, nastiest conk that—"

"What's a conk?"

"An old hairstyle that some less enlightened brothers fell into. It was a way to straighten your hair, but never mind about that."

"Dad, please, what about the money?"

"Steven."

"Yes, Dad?"

"Do you really think the U.S. government would put James Brown on any money?"

"I don't see why not."

"Son, let me tell you, these are trying times for James Brown. I mean, think about it. The rappers are stealing his beats, he hasn't had a hit in decades, and I'm not sure, but I think the last time I saw a picture of him it looked like he was trying to regrow another conk."

"Dad, what does that have to do with my quadrillion-dollar bill?" Steven asked even though he knew the answer.

"It's to prove a point," Dad said.

"What point?"

"It's to prove that I don't know about you some of the time, Steven. Do you honestly think being a musical innovator is going to win you a spot on United States currency?"

"I don't get it, but that bill is only some type of high-tech advertising or stunt or joke that Othello is involved in for some reason. Relax, it's worthless."

"But, Dad, look at it." Steven's voice began to get whiny. He tried to deepen it but it was too late. Once you set down the road to whining there's no turning back. "It's too good to be a joke, it's just—"

"Steven."

"Dad! Look at it, can't you see . . ."

Dad sighed, rolled his eyes and handed Steven back the quadrillion-dollar bill. "Steven."

"Yes, Dad?"

"Scram."

"Yes, Dad" was what Steven said, but he thought, "I'll scram, okay, Mr. Know-It-All-Except-How-to-Grow-Hair-on-Top-of-Your-Head. That's it, you're cut down to one billion dollars, funny man!"

Steven knew he'd have to do some independent research. Maybe the key to the mystery was knowing more about the Godfather of Soul. Steven wasn't an excellent private detective for nothing—he knew right where to get what he needed. It was very dangerous and could cost him his life, or at least get him grounded, but he didn't care. Dad had gone and made the whole thing personal!

SIX

Into the Dungeon!

STEVEN CAREFULLY LOOKED LEFT and listened. Nothing.

He looked right and listened. Nothing again.

He so, so quietly pulled the basement door toward him until it was open. He waited again, listening for the sounds of parents anywhere near. Nothing. He pulled the door shut behind him and tiptoed down into the cool darkness of the basement.

When he got to the bottom of the steps he switched the light on. There before him stood a door with a handwritten sign covering half of it. Dad had printed in capital letters and underlined with red ink,

HALT! FREEZE RIGHT THERE, BUSTER!
Absolutely under no circumstances are you to enter this room. I don't care what happens,

do not, repeat, DO NOT come in here. Don't look at anything beyond this door. If I find out you have been in here I will repossess your fingers. I'M NOT PLAYING WITH YOU, STEVEN DAEMON CARTER. STAY OUT!!!!!!!!!!

Dad had even gone so far as to have Mom add her psychological two cents at the bottom of the sign, just in case that stuff really did work. She'd written, "Steven, I am so proud that you have decided to respect your father's request and will not enter this room. You are making such wonderful progress and your maturity is growing by leaps and bounds."

Steven was very disappointed with the babyish alarm Dad had rigged to the door. It took him less than five seconds to disconnect it.

He shut the door behind him and turned on the overhead light. There it was, shelf after shelf mounted on the walls of the room, the "hands-off" 33-1/3 RPM record album collection! Thousands upon thousands of albums, neatly alphabetized and covered by clear plastic sleeves.

Dad's collection was so famous that every once in a while people would call from New York or some other foreign place and ask questions about some group no one had ever heard of. If Dad didn't know the answer right away he could always go into his record room to get it. He felt great when he could answer each dumb question.

"Oh, well," Steven thought, "little things amuse little minds."

He found the B section of records. Halfway down the shelf he found more than one hundred albums by James Brown.

"It's a wonder he sold any records at all with the terrible names on some of these songs. 'I Got You (I Feel Good)'? 'Papa's Got a Brand New Bag'? 'Cold Sweat'? 'Say It Loud (I'm Black and I'm Proud)'?"

Steven could see what Dad meant about a conk too. In some pictures this James Brown guy had more wavy hair than the Wolfman.

Another strange thing about the Godfather of Soul was that there wasn't one picture on one album that didn't show him without a ton of sweat pouring off him or without his face twisted up like he'd just been poked in the eye. Dad might've been right when he said it wasn't easy being the Godfather of Soul these days, but judging by these pictures it was no piece of cake forty years ago either!

Steven took out the quadrillion-dollar bill and set it next to one of James Brown's albums. Maybe Dad had the right answer here too. Maybe it didn't make much sense for the United States government to print money with the face of such a tired, sweaty man on it, and an African American man on top of it all!

Every other bill had the face of an old dead white president or Founding Father wearing a weird wig or hairdo so why on earth would James Brown fit in with them? It seemed like there would be special rules for putting people on money, it seemed like you'd at least have to be dead.

But maybe Dad wasn't right, maybe this wasn't James

Brown at all. If you squinted your eyes almost shut and held the money off at a distance this guy could be an old dead white president with a really good tan. But that was really stretching it. No, no doubt, this was a picture of James Brown.

Steven pulled out an album called *Live at the Apollo* and began reading the back. Suddenly he gasped—here it was! Part of the mystery was finally solved! The letters *HWMISB* on Mr. Chickee's funny money must stand for the "Hardest-working Man in Show Business"!

Steven felt a little chill run up his neck and tap dance on the hair there. This was becoming too, too scary. Everything was starting to fall into place. The more and more he thought about it the more Steven knew this quadrillion-dollar bill was real! But who could he turn to now to find out what it was worth?

Russell's mom and dad would be no help. Dad's mind was closed on the subject. He couldn't go to the police and even Mr. Chickee was gone for two whole months. There was no way Steven could wait that long.

A smile slowly came to his face. Part of being a great detective was being flexible in your thoughts. If you weren't flexible you ended up like Dad—you made your mind up and that was all, folks! But not the young Mr. Carter, he knew that you had to be able to wiggle around a problem. If you couldn't beat it one way you had to come at it another way.

Steven flexed his mind to the left, then flexed it to the right, then flexed it into a knot. He thought for a very, very,

very long time (well, about five or six seconds anyway) and finally there the answer was, smiling back at him like an old friend. It was time to quit playing around with Mr. Chickee's funny money and get some real answers. It was time to go right to the top. It was time to go to someone with some real authority.

It was time to go to Mom!

SEVEN

Meeting Agent Fondoo (If That's His Real Name!)

STEVEN AND HIS DAD SAT in the waiting room of the Federal Building.

"Look, Steven, get those headphones off your ears, you know better than to wear that MP3 player in here."

Steven just stared at his father.

"Boy," he thought, "I wonder if he has any idea just how predictable he is? I know everything he's going to say before he says it. Maybe volume two of the private eye book *How to Read and Control Strangers' Minds* works on people you know too.

"*Stee-ven!*"

Oops! Steven quickly snatched the headphones from his ears.

"Where do you go some of the time?"

"Sorry, Dad," Steven said, even though he was feeling

anything but. Old Mr. Follow-All-the-Rules hadn't noticed the just about invisible wire that ran from Steven's ear down to the tiny MP3 player on his belt.

Steven almost laughed out loud when he saw that Mr. Act-So-Polite-in-Front-of-Strangers hadn't noticed it wasn't an MP3 player at all but was really a Spyco Elephant Ears Snoopeeze 500 that Steven had secretly, and probably illegally, worked on to make stronger.

He'd discovered that with an extra wire soldered in here and a little fine-tuning there the Snoopeeze 500 became a lot more powerful than it was meant to be. It was now probably a Snoopeeze 2000!

When he'd first put it on after improving it, all he could hear were a lot of booms and crunches, a sound like he was eating Crisped-Out Crunchos for breakfast. He thought he was picking up some strange-sounding static but found out that the sounds were actually made by pieces of dust floating through the air banging into each other! He'd made the Snoopeeze way too sensitive! He adjusted it until people talking far away could be heard without the very distracting sound of ant feet thudding around or the horrible roar of a fly taking off or that creepy creaking sound made by human hair growing.

As Steven looked at Mr. Nothing-Gets-by-Me he smiled again because he knew that with that saucer-sized brown patch of skin on top of Dad's head he'd probably have to do a whole lot more adjusting and strengthening of his Snoopeeze 2000 to hear any hair growing there!

"It's too bad that Afros are back in style," Steven

thought, " 'cause all Dad can grow now is a *Half*-fro." He couldn't help giggling.

"*Steven!*"

Oops. "Yes, Dad?"

"When we get in there you let me explain what's happening. Then you can ask a question or two."

This wasn't what Steven had planned at all. He wanted to impress Dad by harshly questioning the Treasury Department guy they'd come to see and then using rough interrogation techniques to break the man down until he admitted that the quadrillion-dollar bill was real.

Steven frowned and scrunched himself down in his chair. His cross-examination depended on surprising this agent and if Dad ran his mouth first the guy would have a chance to think his answers out or go to his boss to see what he should say. Steven had spent hours and hours . . . well, minutes and minutes . . . okay, a couple of seconds, working on what to say and practicing it in the mirror and now Dad was going to ruin it by talking first.

He wondered if Dad was doing this on purpose, if this was all part of the big payback. Dad had been in a grumpy, resentful mood ever since Steven had gone over his head to Mom.

When Mom had seen Mr. Chickee's funny money she'd been excited by it right away. This was real excitement too, not the kind Mom's last library book, *Dealing with Your Worrisome, Special, Gifted Child* had said she should show about any project or activity Steven came up with.

Steven knew the difference because any book Mom

checked out from the library he'd check out after she'd returned it so he could keep up on all the nonsense or psychological curveballs she'd throw his way. At first he'd been a little bit upset by the description "worrisome, special, gifted child," but two out of three wasn't bad.

"Steven." Mom had looked him right in the eye and put her hand on his shoulder just like the book said she should. "Othello Chickee gave this to you?"

She'd flipped the bill over and over. "This is fascinating! Did you show it to your father yet?"

"He told me to scram." Well, that was part of what Dad had said.

Mom frowned. "Hmmm, I'm going to call Othello and ask him what this is all about."

"You can't, he's gone to Pennsylvania for two or three months."

"Oh, that's right. I'd forgotten he was leaving early this year." Mom rubbed the bill between her thumb and pointing finger. "Steven, this is very unusual. Your interest and sense to know that it requires further looking into are very commendable."

Steven had smiled, but inside his head he'd secretly rolled his eyes. That last line was from the chapter called "Making Your Special One Feel Good About Him- or Herself" in that worrisome kid book.

"What should we do now, Mom?"

"Well, the first thing we're going to do is have your father take a more serious look at this . . . this . . ."

"Quadrillion-dollar bill."

57

"Ah, so that's what it's called. How clever and inquisitive it is of you to have figured this out!"

Mom was stuck on this chapter.

He smiled widely because the book had said, "These children take delight in praise. Heap it on and watch them glow!"

He glowingly said, "Thanks, Mom!"

"Let's go see if your father thinks this bill deserves more than just a 'scram!'"

They walked into the living room, where Dad's face was hidden behind a newspaper.

"Eldren?"

"Hmmm?"

"Look at this."

The newspaper came down and Steven thought, "You have to give the old bird credit, he knew what was going on in a flash."

Dad shot him a quick I'm-gonna-get-you-for-this look and said, "What, dear?"

Mom stuck the bill out at him. "What do you make of this?"

Dad took the bill. "Like I told Steven, I think it's some kind of advertising gimmick. Come on, Lynetta, it can't be real."

"Well," Mom had said, "I'd like a second opinion. There're a lot of things that don't seem right about it and there're a lot of things that do. Don't you think someone downtown at the Treasury Department may have some answers for us?

"It seems to me that this is definitely real currency ink and paper. I'd take him to the Federal Building myself but I've got to work. You were planning on taking Monday off, so why don't you guys have a father and son bonding trip and find out what this is all about?"

Steven wondered if that line had come out of a book called *How to Handle That Boneheaded Husband of Yours.*

Dad said, "A bonding trip?"

He knew Dad would like to bond him to the wall about now.

"Yes, I think that sounds marvelous."

"But, Lynetta, the game is on Mond—"

Steven had fought not to break out laughing then and had to fight not to laugh now as he and his father sat in the eighth-floor waiting room of the Federal Building.

A door that had "Special Agent William T. Fondoo" written on it opened and a tall skinny man came out smiling.

"Mr. Carter? I'm Agent Fondoo, United States Treasury Department."

The man offered his hand to Dad.

"Agent Fondoo, this is my son, Steven."

Steven really enjoyed the times when Dad introduced him to adults this way. It made him look forward to being a grown-up and getting to shake everybody's hand while saying stuff like "Pleased to meet you" or "How ya doing" or especially repeating the person's name—that was going to be his favorite.

"Steven," Fondoo said, "pleased to meet you."

Steven got to say it! "Agent Fondoo, pleased to meet you."

They shook hands and he gave the man a good hard squeeze. No "dead fish" handshakes, Dad always reminded him.

"Ah, a good firm handshake, little fella!" Agent Fondoo said.

He could've left the "little fella" part off but Steven was glad Dad knew he'd crunched the guy's hand.

"Gentlemen, come this way, please."

The man held his office door open and stood aside as Dad and Steven walked in. The office smelled like a bunch of old books and papers.

"Please have a seat."

Across from a small wooden desk were two chairs covered with old brown leather.

The man perched himself on the edge of his desk and said, "Now, how may I help you?"

Agent Fondoo hoped this man and his son couldn't tell how nervous he was. If they had the information he suspected they might have and if he could get it from them then maybe not only could he get his career going again but he'd also be filthy rich. And maybe, just maybe he could get out of Flint too.

He hadn't believed his ears that morning when his secretary, Brad, had come in and said there was a man on the phone who wanted some information on very-high-denomination bills. Agent Fondoo had only moments before thrown out a memo from the Treasury Department director that had the strange heading "Super-Duper Top-Secret If-You-Tell-You'll-Be-in-a-Lot-of-Trouble Special Alert. All Offices Code Chartreuse. $200,000 Reward. Quadrillion-Dollar Bill Warning!"

The memo explained how one of only five existing "extremely high-denomination bills" had accidentally been allowed to get into public circulation. The director said that any government official who was able to get this bill back into federal hands would be awarded two hundred thousand tax-free dollars. The memo had given a special number and code word to use for information and described the bill as "unusual and easily identifiable. It carries the picture of a famous African American soul singer, Mr. James Brown."

Agent Fondoo had said "Phooey" and wadded the memo into a ball. If there really was a bill like that it would never be in Flint and when had his luck been anything but bad?

"Nope," he'd said as he sank two points in the wastebasket with the Super-Duper Top-Secret memo, "not in this lifetime, Billy Boy, maybe next time around. With my luck I'd be happy to find a dime."

But then the unusual call from a Mr. Eldren Carter came in. Could this be more than a coincidence? Agent Fondoo's horoscope that morning had read, "Investigate your hunches. Big payoff in near future, will you be ready?"

Agent Fondoo was indeed ready. He'd even had Brad dust off some high-tech equipment just in case.

Fondoo considered himself an expert at sizing people up

and as he sat on the edge of his desk he knew right away which of these two he should keep his eye on. The father seemed harmless enough but this kid was a different story. There was something about him that Agent Fondoo didn't like.

"So, gentlemen, I believe you said something on the phone about a really, really big piece of money?"

"Well," Dad began, "we have a little problem and a few questions for you, Mr. Fondoo."

"That's why we're here, Mr. Carter, to help in any way we possibly can. Ha ha ha!"

Steven felt a funny little click go off in his head. Whenever that happened it meant that he and his father were thinking exactly the same thing. Right now it was "Uh-oh, this guy's just too smooth, something's up."

Dad's next words made Steven proud of his father.

Dad said, "Maybe Steven should ask our questions."

There was something about this Agent Fondoo that Steven didn't like so he was going to enjoy ripping him apart with some real tricky questions.

He got out of his chair and tried to act like he had a suspect who needed grilling.

"Agent Fondoo," he began. "I can call you Agent Fondoo, can't I?"

Dad groaned. The man laughed and said, "Of course you can, Steven."

"Agent Fondoo, what can you tell us about money?"

The man's forehead wrinkled and he said, "Well, I can tell you I don't make enough, if that's what you mean."

He laughed at his own weak joke and gave Dad a wink. Dad didn't see, though. He had his hand in front of his eyes, fearing Steven's next move.

"Hmmm," Steven thought, "this guy's hiding something." People who joked all the time usually had something up their sleeve.

"No, Agent Fondoo" ("If that's your real name," Steven said to himself), "I mean what do you say is the largest-decombin—" Dad made a choking sound.

Steven corrected himself, "—the largest-denomination bill in U.S. currency?"

"Ah, well, young fella, that is indeed a very good question." Agent Fondoo held his breath and asked, "What do you think is the largest bill that we print?"

Steven hoped Dad's information was correct. He said, "I've always been under the compression that—"

Dad choked again, but so what? Steven was on a roll.

"—that the thousand-dollar bill was the largest bill in general circulation but that there were hundred-thousand-dollar bills that banks transfer among themselves."

A strange look came to Agent Fondoo's face. Steven couldn't tell if the man was surprised by his intelligence or just unhappy about something.

He wasn't too far off. Agent Fondoo was very disappointed. This kid's questions showed he knew nothing about the government's missing money.

This creepy kid was only looking for information so he could do some school project.

"That's exactly right, Steven, and you know what? I'm

gonna get some official United States government pamphlets for you. They explain all about American currency. This is for a school project, huh?"

The man pushed a button on his phone and said, "Brad, could you please bring me a couple of those GPO three-eight-twos?"

Perfect! Steven had Agent Fondoo right where he wanted him. This guy thought Steven was a nosy, stupid, average kid, or as Great-great-grampa Carter's dictionary would put it, maybe even a diminutive dunce. Agent Fondoo obviously thought he was going to get away with dumping some dopey pamphlets printed in 1953 on him.

Then the agent really set himself up. He smiled his fake smile, stood up, stuck his hand out and said, "Thank you for coming in today, you are such a smart little boy. Are there any other questions?"

Steven grabbed the offered hand, blinked his left eye twice and his right eye once and, using a technique from volume two, page four of *How to Read and Control Strangers' Minds*, he began silently counting backward from nine and a half.

"Nine and a half, eight and a half, seven and a half . . ."

Agent Fondoo pumped Steven's hand, still smiling.

"Six and a half, five and a half . . ."

The government guy stared right in Steven's eyes, a really big mistake!

Agent Fondoo thought, "Holy Moses, this is one little nutball here! First he gives me those goofy blinks and now he's got this creepy stare."

Dad had seen enough. He got out of his chair.

"Four and a half, three and a half . . ."

Dad was starting to say something but Steven was able to finish his mental count. He thought just what the book had told him to think: "Two and a half, one and a half, one half, zero! Tennessee Tuxedo!"

Agent Fondoo blinked his right eye twice and his left eye once.

Steven had done it! According to volume two this was the sign that the man's mind was Double Dutch locked! This technique forced whoever it was used on to drool uncontrollably and become extremely confused if they tried to tell a lie.

Steven moved in for the kill. Still shaking Agent Fondoo's hand, he said, "Oh. I do have one more question for you. Whose face is on the quadrillion-dollar bill?"

Bingo!

The man's lower jaw jerked toward the floor. His hand got cold and began shaking under Steven's strong grip.

"The what?" he whispered.

"The quadrillion-dollar bill."

Agent Fondoo couldn't understand why his mouth was suddenly so juicy. He swallowed heavily and said, "Why, uh, let's see now, what was your name? Susan?"

The guy's oily little smile came back and his hand began warming up as he pulled it away from Steven. Good thing too, because as soon as he did a little geyser of drool soaked the front of his shirt.

Steven knew it! Mr. Chickee's funny money wasn't so funny after all!

EIGHT

Great-great-grampa Carter's Dictionary Finally Does Some Good!

AGENT FONDOO TRIED TO KEEP his cool.

"I'm sorry, what was your question?"

"Whose picture is on the quadrillion-dollar bill?"

It all came back to Fondoo. The reward! The special memo! James Brown!

The fog closed in again.

"Uh . . . the largest-decombination bill in the . . . uh . . . United Steaks . . ."

Steven and his dad had to take a step back. Agent Fondoo was drooling like Niagara Falls. Steven's ears were filled with that strange click of Dad having the same thought at the same time: "This guy's lying! He's heard of the quadrillion-dollar bill!" Then they both thought, "Mr. Chickee's funny money is real!"

"Now let's see," Steven thought, "how was I going to divide it? Dad's going to get a half a million, Russell will get two million, Mom'll get . . ."

If Steven had read the entire chapter about Double Dutch Mind-Locking he would've known that the technique can only last for one minute. Agent Fondoo finally got control of his mouth, his drooling glands and his mind and realized he'd better get some more information. He didn't need to get his hopes up for no reason. Maybe this kid didn't know anything about the money after all.

He laughed. "So, who do you think the government would put on a, what did you call it, a quadrillion-dollar bill?" Fondoo held his breath again.

Steven thought, "Now to confuse this guy even more." Some of the time adults were so easy to lead around by their noses, and what could be more fun than leading this sneaky guy and your own father around at the same time?

Steven knew exactly what to say to send Agent Fondoo off the deep end. He'd rehearsed and prepared all night— well, at least for fifteen minutes. All right, once or twice before he dozed off.

And it was all because of Great-great-grampa Carter's rude dictionary.

The night before when he was getting ready for this meeting Steven had looked in the dictionary to find some big impressive words.

He couldn't help himself—he checked out the copyright page first.

The dictionary was still copping an attitude. It said, "What now, Sherlock?"

Steven felt silly doing it, but he told the dictionary everything that had happened and how he needed some big words to confuse Agent Fondoo.

He turned back to the copyright page and read, "The guy's a bureaucrat, huh? (*[BYOOR-e-krat'] n. An official who works by fixed routine without exercising intelligent judgment, or so you'll understand it, A government-type person who does whatever he's told to do without thinking.*) If there's one thing I loathe more than miniature morons such as yourself, it's bureaucrats. I'd be more than happy to help you confuse this government lackey. Let's do this."

Steven looked at Agent Fondoo and cleared his throat like a detective would. "Hmmm, who do I think might be on the quadrillion-dollar bill?"

Steven stood up and put his hand on his chin. "To answer that I'm afraid I'm going to have to use a little *Español* on you, so *por favor, por favor, por favor,* if you'll look carefully you'll notice that I'm in possession of the pronoun of the second person singular and am experiencing a certain mild euphoria. So much so that my pores have erupted in a frigid outpouring of perspiration. Why, you may ask?

"Well, aside from the fact that my parents are of African American heritage, something that has left me feeling greatly pleased and satisfied, and aside from the fact that one of my biological progenitors has recently acquired an unused valise, I have to admit it's time I stopped dallying and applied pressure to the benevolent lower extremity of my vertebral limb. In other words, Agent Fondoo, relax your grip on it, cede it."

Agent Fondoo looked at Dad and Dad looked at Agent Fondoo.

"Man," Steven thought, "adults look so ridiculous with their mouths wide open and their eyes bugging out of their heads."

Dad collapsed back into his chair and Fondoo slid around to his seat, kind of like he wanted to get some distance between Steven and himself.

Steven thought he'd better finish his speech before one of them told him to put a cork in it.

"You see, it's like I said the other day: Matriarch, approach me with haste and deliver unto me that crude instrument of corporal punishment."

Agent Fondoo stared blankly at Steven. Dad was making little sobby sounds. Steven saw he'd better finish this up.

"Quite shocking, isn't it? I was minding my own business when a member of the class *Insecta*, family *Formicidae*, juxtaposed itself into my trousers and triggered a great urge for me to rhythmically move my body to a musical beat."

He was so proud of himself that his ears started wiggling all on their own. He leaned across the desk until his face was inches away from the government guy's. "Does that answer your question, Agent Fondoo? Is that ringing any bells? Will you tell us now whose picture is on the quadrillion-dollar bill?"

You didn't need a Snoopeeze 2000 to hear what was going on after Steven stopped speaking. Dad's hands were back covering his face and his head was shaking from side to side as he mumbled, "Why? Why'd I listen to his mother? Why'd I bring him up here? I knew I should've stayed in the car, I knew it would end up like this, with him going nutso in public. Why? Why? Why?"

With every word that Steven had spoken Fondoo's smile had grown greasier and greasier and he'd had to fight the urge to break out laughing in this babbling kid's face.

"Darn!" Agent Fondoo thought. "To think I really believed that someone would come in here knowing about the missing money. It was obvious that this kid wasn't operating on all cylinders as soon as he opened his mouth.

"*Por favor, por favor, por favor,* how can I hurry up and get this little wacko out of my office? He's triggered a great urge for me to take a couple of weeks' vacation.

"And what's the deal with this kid's ears? They're flapping like a flag in a hurricane!"

Steven knew he had to get his father involved or all his memorizing and all the help of Great-great-grampa Carter's bad-attitude dictionary were headed down the drain.

"Well, Agent Fondoo, since it seems you're having trouble understanding, perhaps my father can help translate."

Dad didn't look like he could help anything. He looked like he was in shock.

This disappointed Steven. Dad could be a pain, but he was supposed to be a smart pain.

"Man," Steven thought, "don't tell me I took all that lip from that dictionary for nothing. Maybe instead of reading it I should've ordered that time machine out of the comic book and gone back in time and had Mom marry a different guy."

Steven looked as hard as he could at his father and said, "Dad, would you translate, please? *Por favor, por favor, por favor* . . ."

Suddenly Dad's mouth closed, his eyes cleared and an itsy-bitsy flicker of intelligence came to them.

"Wait a minute," Dad said, "there's a method to this madness! *Por favor, por favor, por favor* is 'Please, Please, Please,' released on November 6, 1955, went to number six on the soul charts!"

Steven breathed a sigh of relief. Dad finally got it!

Steven repeated, "I'm in possession of the pronoun of the second person singular and I'm in a state of mild euphoria . . ."

Dad closed his eyes and thought for a second before he said, " 'I Got You (I Feel Good),' released November 11, 1965, reached number one on the soul charts and number two on the Top Forty!"

Steven grinned and said, "My pores erupt in a frigid outpouring of perspiration?"

Dad laughed, "Easy, 'I break out in a cold sweat'—'Cold Sweat,' released July 22, 1967, number one on the soul charts, number ten on the Top Forty!"

Steven said, "Exclaim blaringly, my parents are African

American in heritage, a fact that leaves me greatly pleased and satisfied?"

Dad balled up his fist, raised it over his head and shouted, " 'Say It Loud (I'm Black and I'm Proud)'! Released September of 1968, number one on soul, number seventeen on pop, which I've never understood."

Steven, "Apply pressure to the beneficial extremity of the vertebral limb?"

Dad, " 'Get On the Good Foot,' released September 9, 1972, number one on the soul charts, number eighteen on the less enlightened pop charts."

Steven, "Matriarch, approach with haste and deliver unto me that crude instrument of corporal punishment?"

Dad, "I was kind of hoping we could skip this one, Steven, I don't have the slightest idea."

Steven said, "Come on, Dad, break it down in smaller pieces and think it out. What is a matriarch?"

"A mother?"

Steven said, "Very good. Now reason the next part carefully. What does 'approach with haste' sound like it means?"

Dad's face twisted. "I don't know."

Steven reached over and thunked the bald spot on Dad's head.

"Come on, Dad, think!" Thunk!

Dad said, "Uh, uh, uh . . ."

Thunk!

Dad said, "Could it mean 'come here quickly'?"

"Very good!" Steven said. "And what is a crude instrument of corporal punishment?"

"A whipping stick?"

"Close."

"A spanking stick?"

Thunk!

"A licking stick!"

"Put it together and what have you got?"

" 'Mama, come here quick, and bring me that licking stick'—'Licking Stick,' number one soul and number sixteen pop. Released May of 1968!"

Steven, "Several members of the family *Formicidae* have juxtaposed themselves into my trousers, which has triggered a great urge for me to rhythmically move my body to a musical beat?"

" 'I Got Ants in My Pants (And I Want to Dance)'! Released January of seventy-three, number one soul, number thirty-three pop!"

Steven, ". . . and finally, residing in these United States."

Dad began singing, off-key of course, " 'Living in America, yee-ow! Coast to coast, station to station . . .' Theme from *Rocky IV*, released January of eighty-six, number one on the soul charts, and, aww, who cares about the Top Forty? Number one across the nation!"

Dad and Steven hugged. Agent Fondoo leaned back in his chair and thought, "At least I can see where the kid gets his looniness from, it's inherited. I'd better call Security to get these nuts outta here." But just as he was about to press the red emergency button under his desk the older nut said, "And who was it who released these songs, Steven? Who was that masked man?"

73

The little nut laughed and said, "Was it the Godfather of Soul?"

The big nut answered, "Uh-huh, was it the hardest-working man in show business?"

Little nut, "Sure was. Was it soul brother number one, Mr. Entertainment?"

Big nut, "Sounds like it to me!"

Both nuts together, "Was it the man on the quadrillion-dollar bill?"

Little nut, "You bet it was."

Big nut, "And I repeat, who, my dear son, who was that masked man?"

Both nuts together again, imitating rap records, "Ja-Ja-Ja-Ja-James Brown!"

Agent Fondoo didn't know why but before he could stop himself he jumped up on the top of his desk, did a very painful split, bounced right back up, thought, "I cain't hep mysef!" and screamed, "Yeee-oww!"

He fell back in his chair and broke out in a cold sweat!

NINE

The Ponytail Patriots

"GENTLEMEN, GENTLEMEN, PLEASE BE SEATED. Brad will be right in with those pamphlets."

Steven and Dad exchanged looks as Agent Fondoo limped to the door and said, "I'll be just a moment, I want to see what's keeping Brad."

Steven could swear he heard a click as the door was locked from the outside. Dad didn't seem to notice so Steven thought he might've imagined it. Finally Dad said, "I'm not sure what's going on here, but something is definitely fishy."

Dad was an expert at smelling out fishy situations. "Let's calm down and be patient and find out what this agent has to say," he went on. "Maybe that quadrillion-dollar bill is worth something after all." Dad looked over at Steven and sighed. Steven wasn't paying attention again, he'd drifted off somewhere in his own thoughts.

This was exactly what Steven wanted Dad to believe. He stared out into space hoping his father would just be quiet. Sometimes adults spent too much time saying things everybody already knew. Although Steven was looking spacy and acting spacy he was actually quite busy and focused on what he was doing.

What Dad couldn't see was that Steven's right hand was furiously twisting and fine-tuning the dials on the side of his specially modified Snoopeeze 2000. If Dad would just quiet down for a minute Steven was sure his secret device would be able to pick up whatever conversation Agent Fondoo was having with the mysterious Brad in the next room.

Dad gave Steven that sad look he got whenever he thought his son had drifted away.

"It's about time!" Steven thought.

The almost invisible earphone began picking up Agent Fondoo's voice.

". . . direct to headquarters in Washington, Brad, on the supersecret line. When you get ahold of the director I'll need privacy so go get us a couple of coffees and get me a big bag of ice, I think I've pulled some muscles."

Steven heard the numbers being punched into a telephone, then Brad's voice. "Thank you. Code quatro-digit-seven-two-sixer. That is correct, this is Code Chartreuse.

"Agent Fondoo, I've reached the director in Washington."

Steven could hear Fondoo whisper, "Just one minute, Madam Director, this is Code Chartreuse and my office is not secured as of yet.

"Brad, could you go get those coffees and the ice now, please? I think I'm feeling some swelling already."

The Snoopeeze 2000 picked up the sound of the front office door closing, then, "Yes, ma'am, I'm very serious, this is Code Chartreuse."

Pause.

"Correct, the subjects are two African American males, apparently a father and son. The kid says his name is Steven—I'm not sure I believe him, though."

Pause.

"Yes, yes, they seem to be aware that the item exists, they provide a pretty accurate description."

Pause.

"No, ma'am, I have not actually seen it, I thought my first move should be to contact you."

Pause.

"I'm not really sure, ma'am, but yes, there is a possibility that they could be secret agents, the kid especially. The father seems a bit slow, but that kid! He talks like a dictionary sometimes, and his eyes! I've dealt with master spies and supersecret agents all over the world but this kid's got the scariest eyes I've ever seen. For a second there it seemed like he actually had control of my mind!

"It reminded me of the time I was captured on the Island of Boom-Chaka-Lakalaka by their king of mind control and he made me eat dirt and bugs for three days in a row, then—"

The Snoopeeze 2000 picked up a woman's voice from Washington shouting, "Agent Fondoo! That is quite enough. Have you forgotten why you were transferred to Flint in the first place? You simply must stop telling people those horrid Island of Boom-Chaka-Lakalaka stories, they're so boring that they could . . ."

The woman toned her voice down and Steven couldn't hear the end of what she was saying.

Finally Agent Fondoo said, "Sorry, Madam Director, it's just that this kid's eyes are so creepy and when he started using all those big words it left me very confused."

Pause.

"Yes, ma'am. I'm having both of their identities and files run through the NSA, the CIA, the FBI, the IRS, the A&P, and the EIEIO. The reports should be back within the next hour."

Pause.

"Yes, I realize the absolute importance of getting the item back."

Pause.

"I know all about the two-hundred-thousand-dollar reward. I may even offer them a portion of it if I can't get them to surrender the item in any other way."

Pause.

"Yes, ma'am, I'm well aware that I've messed things up before but let me assure you that I won't fumble this time!

78

Thank you for trusting me, Madam Director, I won't let you down. I'll be back in touch with you as soon as I have any more information. Code Chartreuse over and out."

Steven switched the Snoopeeze 2000 off and wondered what he should do. A portion of two hundred thousand dollars could be a lot of money, but it was still a drop in the bucket compared to a quadrillion dollars. Maybe he should tell Dad what he knew, but how on earth could he let Dad know what was going on without showing him the Snoopeeze 2000? Dad would just think Steven's mind and imagination were drifting away again and wouldn't take him seriously.

"Steven," Dad said, "I've made up my mind."

Uh-oh!

"I'll bet you anything that this quadrillion-dollar bill is some type of experimental trial that the Treasury Department has run. That Agent Fondoo guy obviously knew what we were talking about and was shaken up by the fact that we knew about it."

Dad cleared his throat. Through many years of experience Steven had learned that when Dad was scolding him he could tune out all his father's negative and depressing words until he heard the "her-herm" sound of his father's throat being cleared. If Dad asked any questions they usually only involved information that came right after that horrible sound. It was important to be alert then so you didn't just automatically answer Dad's scolding questions by saying "Yes, Dad."

Steven couldn't forget that lesson since the time Dad had been scolding him then had asked something and Steven had said, "Yes, Dad," and Dad had hit the roof. Steven found out later that his father had asked, "Steven, do you think I'm out of my mind?"

Now Dad was "her-herm"ing again so Steven knew he had to pay attention.

"Her-herm, so the only thing I can possibly see is that while this quadrillion-dollar bill is printed by the Treasury Department it was most likely part of someone's experiment done to test a new printing process.

"Or it might be a part of something that went too far and was released accidentally to the public somehow. I've heard that these Treasury agents are quite well known for their great sense of humor and their many practical jokes.

"So, while it can't possibly have any real monetary value, maybe it's worth quite a bit as a collector's item. Maybe, just maybe, if we put it away for a couple of years it might someday be worth . . . now, I don't want you to get too excited by this, but it might actually be worth two or three hundred dollars!"

"Oh, no!" Steven thought. "Dad's going to sell out too cheap!"

He couldn't help himself—he yelled out, "But, Dad! It's real! It's a real quadrillion-dollar bill! It's worth exactly one quadrillion dollars! Not two hundred dollars! Not two thousand dollars! Not even two million dollars! They know about it in Washington! Madam Director said there's a two-hundred-thousand-dollar reward for it! It's real, hard, stone-cold, honest-to-goodness—"

"Steven!"

"Yes, Dad?" Uh-oh, the whining voice was coming back.

"That's it, young man. Listen, I have to admit you did an excellent job of questioning Agent Fondoo but now is the time more experienced minds have to take over. You've done very well, but trust me, I know what I'm doing, agreed?"

Real low Steven said, "Yes, Dad." But he thought, "I know what I'd like to agree to do, I'd like to go to the bathroom and readjust this Snoopeeze 2000 into about a Snoopeeze 10,000, then I'd like to agree to come back and tell Dad that I'd discovered an old Temptations album and had downloaded it on my MP3 for him, then when he put the headphones on I'd turn the volume on that baby up to level 10 and sneak up behind him and slap that bald spot and watch when the sound waves hit him so hard that his brain would jump out of his ear and run around on the floor yelping like a sick puppy!"

"Gentlemen!" Agent Fondoo came back into his office. It looked like he'd pumped two more quarts of oil into his greasy smile. "Here's your pamphlet, Steven."

On its cover was a drawing of a talking dollar bill saying "I'm Bunky, the wonderful dollar bill, where do I come from? The story of United States currency."

Agent Fondoo said, "Now, little fella, why don't you tell me more about this, ha ha, quadrillion-dollar bill?"

Steven said, "There's really not a whole lot to—"

Dad interrupted. "Yes, Agent Fondoo, there's really not a whole lot to say, you know how children's imaginations are. Comes from too much TV, I'd guess, maybe too much sugar, you know the drill."

Dad stood up. Steven followed his lead. Agent Fondoo looked panic-stricken.

"Well, well, well, you aren't leaving so quickly, are you? I was just beginning to enjoy our conversation. In fact I was just about to—"

Dad said, " 'Fraid we have to hit the road, Agent Fondoo, I've got several projects that need my attention and I don't think Steven has practiced his saxophone or done all his chores yet today, have you, son?"

"No, Dad," Steven grumbled. He thought, "Parents! If I could find someone else who'd give me free food and clothes and toys and a place to stay I'd be outta here like a shot!"

Agent Fondoo said, "Here, why don't each of you take one of my cards? If you do hear anything more about that, ha ha, bill, why don't you give me a call? Who knows, there might even be a substantial reward for it, ha ha."

This grabbed Dad's attention and he nudged Steven with his elbow, like he was saying, "See! I told you so!"

"Really?" Dad said. "And exactly how would you define *substantial?*"

"Hmmm." Agent Fondoo scratched his chin like he was thinking real deep. "I believe we're talking about something in the range of, oh, two thousand dollars!"

Dad looked like he was about to shout, "Two thousand dollars!"

"Oh, no!" Steven thought. "He's going to blow this, he's thinking about how many record albums two thousand dollars can buy!"

"Her-herm, her-herm," Dad said when he'd recovered enough to speak, "we'll keep that figure in mind."

Dad stuck Agent Fondoo's card in his front pocket. "We'll give you a call in a day or two, maybe we'll know something by then."

Agent Fondoo's smile showed way too many teeth and his voice became very low. "Yes, Mr. Carter, that would be very wise. Who knows what might happen? There are strange accidents every day, aren't there?"

Steven straightened up. Clark Elementary had a zero-tolerance rule on threats and that sure was a big one! It was time to take scientific action against this guy.

He strained to remember—he thought it was page five of *How to Read and Control Strangers' Minds*, from a chapter called "Involuntary Body Part Migrations, or IBPMs."

This had been Steven's favorite part of the book and he'd studied it for months. Well, not really for months, but a couple of hours anyway. Well, he was pretty sure he'd read it twice.

There was a warning on the front page that read, "IBPMs should only be used against the most evil people you know. The author cannot be held responsible if Involuntary Body Part Migrations are used on someone and the results aren't exactly perfect."

Wow! This was some real serious stuff, serious enough to be used on some government guy who was making threats against Dad.

The book had said that the easiest part of the human anatomy to migrate involuntarily was the mouth and that the easiest direction in which to migrate it was from south to north.

"In just a few minutes, Agent Fondoo," Steven thought, "you'll have to part the hair on the top of your head to brush your teeth!"

"Agent Fondoo!" Steven yelled. "Look!"

The government guy looked down at Steven. Steven shut his left eye halfway and left his right eye halfway open. He stared directly at the last hair on Agent Fondoo's right eyebrow and, just like the book told him to do, he began counting double backward from twenty-four to himself, "Ruof-ytnewt, eerht-ytnewt, owt-ytnewt, eno-ytnewt . . ."

Even before Agent Fondoo's lips had involuntarily migrated past his nose Dad grabbed Steven's arms and pulled him out the door.

As they waited for the elevator Dad said, "Listen, young man, you've got to stop weirding out like that in public. Do you understand me?"

Steven looked at his shoes and said, "Yes, Dad."

In the elevator Dad blurted out, "That thing is worth a lot more than I thought. If he offered us two thousand dollars right off the bat like that, then it must be worth somewhere around three thousand dollars! With a little shrewd negotiating on my part we might even get him to jack up the reward to four thousand dollars!

"I could pay some bills and still have enough left over to buy that original, mint-condition, first-pressing, white-label Billy Stewart album from Technology's Passed You By Records, one of only three hundred twenty-eight known to exist. I bet I could get them to drop the price down to four or five hundred dollars. Do you have any idea how long I've wanted to get my hands on that . . ."

Dad was lost in Album Land. Steven knew it was time to make his final and most important move.

When they got outside the Federal Building he pulled his MP3 player off his belt, slipped it into his pocket, slapped his forehead and said, "Dad, I left my MP3 up in that guy's office, can I go back and get it?"

"What? Oh, yeah—hurry, though, and don't say another word to him if you see him. I'll pull the car around."

"Yes, Dad."

Steven ran back into the building. When the elevator opened on the eighth floor he stuck his head out the door to make sure Agent Fondoo or Brad wasn't in the hall.

The coast was clear. Steven tiptoed past the front door and walked into a closet that was right next to the Treasury Department's office.

When he got inside and pulled the door shut behind him he began twisting the knobs on his Snoopeeze 2000 until he heard Agent Fondoo's voice.

". . . that is correct, Washington, Code Chartreuse. For the director's ears only."

There was a pause, then, "Hello, Madam Director, Special Agent Fondoo here again."

Steven turned up the Snoopeeze 2000 to the maximum level and pressed it right against the wall. He heard a woman say, ". . . Fondoo. Do you have any more information?"

"Um, nothing affirmative to report on that, ma'am. I do have some questions, though."

"Well?"

"First of all, what's the deal with this quadrillion-dollar bill? In all our pamphlets Bunky, the Wonderful Talking Dollar Bill, has always said that the one-hundred-thousand-dollar bill is the largest in U.S. currency. He hasn't been lying all this time, has he?"

Steven could hear the sigh all the way from Washington. The director finally said, "Fondoo, those pamphlets were written in 1953. Two years ago the national debt got so high that we secretly had to print a few quadrillion-dollar bills to cover payments within the government."

Fondoo said, "Well, if it was done secretly how did this one get out in the public?"

"We're not sure, but since we had to blame someone we've chosen an Agent Malaney. By the way, she'll be your new aide in Flint by the end of the month."

"Okay, Madam Director, now for my big question. How in the world did James Brown get on the quadrillion-dollar bill?"

Another long sigh came from Washington. "Fondoo, I'm only going to explain it once so you'd better listen very carefully."

"Yes, Madam Director."

"OK. There were five and a half pages of the United States Constitution that weren't discovered until the mid-eighteen hundreds. Two of the pages had to do with secret rules for printing money. There were over forty rules and regulations for the size, color, weight and shape of dollar bills. Over half of these rules dealt very specifically with whose picture could go on the currency.

"The rules established a special commission to choose that person and gave painfully detailed qualifications to follow."

Agent Fondoo interrupted. "But how could those qualifications come up with James Brown?"

"This is superduper top-secret but since you've apparently located one of the bills I suppose you have a right to know."

"Thank you, ma'am."

"It seems that not only were the writers of the Constitution landlords, farmers and lawyers, they were also . . ."

There was a long pause. ". . . They were also cosmetologists, aestheticians and hairstylists."

Agent Fondoo yelled, "They were what?"

"Fondoo, if you interrupt me one more time you'll be back on the Island of Boom-Chaka-Lakalaka so fast your head will spin."

"Oops."

"Yes, they were cosmetologists, aestheticians and hair-stylists. Ben Franklin was the first Doo-Master General. Betsy Ross not only sewed the first flag, she also invented the process of hair weaves. And Jefferson apparently wouldn't answer anyone unless they called him Mr. Tomás.

"Of course they weren't called cosmetologists or aestheticians or hairstylists back then. Our research seems to indicate they were called . . ."

Another long pause. "Among themselves they were known as the Ponytail Patriots."

Fondoo couldn't help himself. "Say it ain't so, Madam Director, say it ain't so!"

"They were very, very dedicated to good hair care and the freedom of what they referred to as 'expressive tresses.' They felt that a beautifully coiffed head of hair was a metaphor for freedom, justice and the American way and thought it should always be rewarded and recognized. Apparently they felt that the ultimate reward and recognition was to have your hairstyle immortalized on American currency."

Agent Fondoo could be heard openly sobbing. "But James Brown?"

"Yes, James Brown. There's a rare photograph taken of Mr. Brown back in 1957 that shows him with a particular hairstyle that was somewhat popular among less enlightened members of our community at that time. It was called a conk.

"To make a long story longer, this hairdo worn by James

Brown has been the only one since Lincoln that has met all the criteria set out by the Ponytail Patriots. James Brown's 1957 hairdo symbolized American growth in all directions at once, so we had no choice but to put his likeness on the new quadrillion-dollar bill."

"But, Madam Director, I thought you had to be a dead president, perkily styled hairdo or not."

"Many people operate under that misconception, Fondoo, but remember, Ben Franklin and Alexander Hamilton weren't presidents.

"As far as being dead, you're right, you are supposed to be dead before your face goes onto money, but no one at the Treasury Department had heard anything about James Brown in quite some time so we all assumed he was dead. Like it or not, that's the story. James Brown is on the quadrillion-dollar bill and that's that. Besides, the man is a true American genius, have you ever really listened to the lyrics of 'I Got Ants in My Pants (And I Want to Dance)'?"

"No, I guess I never have."

"I thought not. You shouldn't criticize Mr. Brown until you've walked a mile in his shoes. The man is a legend."

"I guess I've never really given him enough credit."

"You're right."

"So is this bill really worth anything to these guys? I mean, they can't just go out and spend it, can they?"

"Of course they can! All they have to do is take it to any local bank and turn it in and they're instant quadrillionaires. That's why it's so important for you to get it back. That's why we we're offering the enormous reward, that's why you simply must . . ."

Steven couldn't hear the rest of the woman from Washington's words. His heart had started beating so loud and hard and fast that all the Snoopeeze 2000 was picking up was "Lub-dub! Lub-dub! Lub-dub!"

Agent Fondoo's next words didn't do a thing to slow Steven's heart down. "Yes, ma'am. I gave them a couple of my cards and a pamphlet all treated with special tracking ink. We'll be able to follow them anywhere they go and when the special ink comes within two feet and three inches of the quadrillion-dollar bill it will trigger a top-secret transmitter and we'll be able to move in and recover it."

Steven's heart began beating even louder. "LUB-DUB! LUB-DUB! LUB-DUB!"

Agent Fondoo said, "We'll give them twenty-four hours to turn the item in and collect the two thousand dollars. If they haven't done it by that time we'll recover that quadrillion-dollar bill *by any means necessary!*"

Threats again! Steven swallowed hard. He'd read enough comic books and seen enough movies to know what "by any means necessary" meant.

"LUB-DUB! LUB-DUB! LUB-DUB!"

Agent Fondoo sounded very cheery. "Great! Yes, ma'am. Oh! There is one other thing, Madam Director, something on a personal level that you may find amusing. I'm not sure why, but I just noticed I can darn near stick half my tongue in my left nostril! Isn't that strange? I've never been able to do that before and suddenly it's like my tongue has gotten longer or like my nose has moved down closer to my mouth! Or maybe . . ."

Steven had to plug his ears. The director screamed so loud that the Snoopeeze 2000 actually started shaking!

"Agent Fondoo!" the director screamed. "Close your mouth this instant! I don't find the length of your tongue the least bit interesting! You get that quadrillion-dollar bill back or I'll not be responsible for where you're transferred next.

"By the way, Fondoo, I've been dying to introduce you to a dear friend of mine. Agent Fondoo, meet Mr. Click."

Steven heard the phone go click as the director hung up and Agent Fondoo said, "Hello? Hello? Hello?"

Finally he said, "Brad, could you come in here for a moment, please?"

"Yes, sir?"

"Watch this, Brad. Can you do this with your tongue and your left nostril?"

"Uh, no, sir, I don't believe I can. Maybe if I practiced. Is this close?"

Agent Fondoo said, "Not really. I just can't understand why all of a sudden . . ."

Steven had heard enough. He pulled the headphones off his ears and ran down the eight flights of stairs to Dad. Dad was still mumbling about Billy Stewart albums and as they drove away Steven looked out the back window, wondering which of the cars behind them was there to follow them home and which of the hundreds of antennae on top of the Federal Building was tuned in to the stupid cards Agent Fondoo had given them and to Bunky, the Wonderful Talking Dollar Bill.

Steven said, "Dad! I just had a great idea! Why don't we just turn around and go back to the Federal Credit Union and open an account and deposit the quadrillion-dollar bill in it and just see what happens after that?"

But it was no use, Dad had turned the radio to W Three Soul, Flint's moldy-oldy station, and they were playing a song by some million-year-old group called Parliament. Dad's mind was gone and he didn't hear a word his son had to say.

But what was worse, whenever one of these old-school groups came on Dad would make anyone who was riding in the car "get in the groove" and bounce and wave their arms along with the music. You also had to sing the chorus with Dad. You did it or you walked.

As the Carters' car turned left onto Wellington Street Steven and his father waved their arms, bobbed their heads and sang,

"Wa-ha-he-he need the funk, gotta have that funk!"

And even though Steven looked like he had gotten the funk and was deep into the groove he really was thinking about what he should do next.

"Boy, oh boy," Steven thought, "I'ma have to do some extra serious reasoning this time!"

TEN

Busted!

STEVEN TOOK THE CHAIR FROM the front of his closet door and put it next to his bed. This one little move changed the room from his bedroom into his office. A very messy, untidy, unkempt office, but still an office. If he wanted the room to become his living room he just would move that same chair next to the other two chairs against the wall and spread a blanket over them to make them a couch. But now he was in big need of an office, he had some very heavy-duty thinking to do and not much time to do it.

He stared down at the Bunky, the Wonderful Talking Dollar Bill pamphlet and began debating himself on how he should handle Agent Fondoo's tricky tracking ink.

"Maybe if I flushed Bunky down the toilet they'd go on a wild-goose chase to get him back!

"Nah, they'd have enough sense to just go straight to the Flint River to find Bunky.

"Maybe I could tie him to a helium balloon and let him go in the next tornado we have!

"Nah, they'd only have to look in the nearest trailer park for Bunky.

"Maybe I could tie Bunky to Zoopy's tail when he goes out on one of his morning adventures!

"Nah, most of the times Zoopy's morning adventures don't take him any farther away than the Woodses' front porch for his first nap of the day."

There was a tap at Steven's window.

It was Russell.

Steven opened the window.

"Heya, Bucko. Did you get us any cash yet?"

"Heya, Russell. No, I've got a real problem with the quadrillion-dollar bill." Steven didn't know how much he should tell Russell about what had happened at the Federal Building. Not only was Russell terrible at keeping secrets, he also didn't understand much about being a detective or using detective tools.

When Steven had first gotten his new Snoopeeze 500 he'd taken it over to Russ's house to show him how it worked. Russell asked if he could borrow it for a second and when Steven handed it to him Russ pulled up his shirt and put the black box on his stomach.

"Russell, what are you doing, trying to listen to your heart?"

"Nope, Bucko. Whenever I get hungry my stomach always starts growling at me so I figured out if I could hear exact-ally what it was saying then I could save a whole lotta time not having to guess what it wants me to feed it. Pretty smart, huh, Bucko? See, I'ma be a detective just like you when I grow up!"

Steven decided he'd better give Russell the second-grade version of what had happened at the Federal Building.

"It seems like there are some bad people who want to get ahold of Mr. Chickee's funny money, Russ. We've got to figure out a way to stop them from getting it."

"No problem, mon," Russell said. Some of the time Russell liked showing his Jamaican roots by imitating his father's voice. "Don't forget, we've got a secret weapon, Bucko, we've got Zoopy!"

"Yeah, Russell, how could anyone forget Zoopy? I was just trying to figure out a way we could use him to keep those people away from our cash."

"I guess that means I should start exercising him to fight bad guys, huh, Bucko?"

"That's a great idea, Russ, it looks like we're going to need all the help we can get."

"See you later, Agent Bucko."

"See you later, Agent Russell."

Steven closed his bedroom window, kind of glad that Russell was gone so he could get back to some serious, adult-type detective thinking.

"Hmmm," Steven thought, "maybe I could catch a bird

and tie this pamphlet to its tail and it might migrate to Japan or somewhere.

"Nah. I've been trying to catch a bird for almost nine years and I've never even gotten close. Besides, tying a stupid government pamphlet to a bird's tail might be cruel."

Steven sighed. All this secret agent stuff was way too exciting.

He walked over to his safe, disarmed the special pepper alarm and pulled out one of his experimental tennis shoes. He pulled the shoe's tongue back and reached into the secret compartment he'd sewn in. The quadrillion-dollar bill was still safe inside.

He pulled the bill out and sat back down at his table.

"Man, I can't believe one piece of money can cause so much trouble and worry. I'm really getting sick of this."

Steven smacked his forehead with his hand. He did that some of the time when a really good idea had sneaked into his brain and was just about to sneak back out. Smacking his forehead kind of stunned the idea for a second, which gave him more time to think about it before it got away.

"Wow!" Steven said. "Why didn't I think of this before? I don't need Mom or Dad to take me downtown to the bank, I can do it myself! Madam Director did say if I cashed it at a bank I'd be an instant quadrillionaire!"

Steven set the bill on his table and went to the closet to get a real pair of shoes.

As soon as he bent over to dig the shoes out the danger bell went off in his head. He jerked straight up. The danger bell only went off when he'd just made a really gigantic, super-bonehead mistake.

He turned around and looked at his table and his mouth flew open when he saw what'd he'd just done: there on the table was the quadrillion-dollar bill and very close to it was the Bunky the Wonderful Talking Dollar Bill pamphlet, the one with the special tracking ink that would set off an alarm in Agent Fondoo's office if it got within two feet and three inches of Mr. Chickee's funny money!

Boom! Boom! Boom!

Someone with a very heavy, official-sounding knock was banging on the front door!

Steven jumped into his shoes, grabbed his quadrillion-dollar bill and climbed out his window, landing on top of Mom's geraniums.

"Uh-oh," Steven said. "Oh, well, I'll buy her all of Geranium Land when I cash this bill in. Now I've got to get to the bank and open an account!"

He shot toward the alley that ran behind his house. No secret federal agents could possibly know Steven's neighborhood as well as he did, and even if they had top-secret maps of the alley they'd never be able to squeeze through the cracks in the fences and holes in the garages the way he could. All he had to do was get into that alley!

Steven was going full speed. Just as he was about to push the backyard gate open he heard a man shout, "Out back, Agent Two! The subject has the item and is making a break through the backyard!"

Steven turned to see two men in black suits running toward him, both pointing something in his direction. He pushed the gate and exploded into the alley. Just as he turned to head down to the Maneys' garage and safety he ran into something that blacked out the sky and knocked him flat on his back gasping for air.

When his head cleared he looked up expecting to see the two government guys standing over him with handcuffs. Instead it looked like the entire sky had turned bright pink.

Steven opened his mouth to say, "What in the wor—"

Something wet and warm and kind of salty smothered his entire face.

"Yack!" It was Zoopy, saying hi.

Russell stood next to his dog laughing his head off. The two agents ran into the alley, each carrying a small satellite dish that was beeping loudly. When they saw Steven lying on his back wiping his tongue on his shirt they smiled at each other.

The Treasury Department must give these guys their smiles because both men had the same greasy grin that Agent Fondoo had.

Agent One said, "Well, hello, son. Decide to take a nap? Excuse us for disturbing you but we'd like to know if you'd mind having a quick chat with us?"

Agent Two had a much meaner voice. "We have reason to believe you may be holding some government property, kid, how about handing it over before we have to—"

Agent One interrupted. "Now, now," he said, still smiling the oily smile, "no need for talk like that, is there, son? All we want is that item that isn't yours. How about it?"

The agents had been so busy watching Steven that they hadn't even noticed Zoopy and Russell. Zoopy wasn't used to being ignored and didn't like the mean way these guys were talking to his friend so he let out two of his mightiest woofs.

"*Ah-oof! Ah-oof!*"

Windows shook, the ground started wiggling and Steven and Russell put their hands over their ears. Once Zoopy started woofing you never knew when he'd stop.

Agent One screamed, "It's alive! I thought it was a car!" He threw his satellite dish at Zoopy and backed up against the Carters' fence.

Agent Two squeezed his dish so hard that it crumbled into four pieces before he threw it down and ran over to where Agent One stood shaking next to the fence.

Both men had their hands up in front of them like they were expecting Zoopy to pounce.

Agent One said, "Watch the animal, son. Be a good boy and call him back."

Agent Two kept repeating, ". . . nice bear, nice bear, nice bear . . ."

Steven saw his chance to escape. He jumped to his feet and looked up the alley toward the Maneys' house but a brown car that had a sign on the door saying SECRET GOVERNMENT CAR pulled up and blocked that end of the alley off.

Agents Three and Four were just getting out of the car and slowly started walking toward them.

Steven looked down the alley toward the Woodses' house but again there was an identical car totally blocking that way out. Agents Five and Six stood there with their little satellite dishes beeping away. The members of the Flint Future Detectives Club were completely surrounded!

"Oh, no," Steven thought, "what would a real detective do to solve this problem? These guys are going to find out any second that Zoopy is a big sweetie and when they do they're just going to hold me down and take the money from me."

Agent One eased a little bit away from the fence and, keeping one eye on Zoopy, tried to grab Steven's arm.

Steven remembered a scene like this from his favorite karate movie, *The Five Wiggly Fingers of Death*. A bunch of evil ninjas had surrounded the hero in an alley and were going to break him into a skillion pieces. The hero got away by doing a quadruple backflip and landing on top of a house. Steven judged that the roof of the Maneys' garage was only about fourteen feet high and that he'd only need to do a triple backflip to reach it.

Old Mr. Spoil-Everything-That-He-Doesn't-Believe-Is-True Dad had said that these movies were nothing but special effects and phoniness but Steven knew if you were scared enough you could do just about anything. And as scared as he was right now Steven could probably do a quaziple backflip fifty feet into the air!

He leaned his body backward, closed his eyes for concentration and kicked his legs harder than he'd ever kicked them before.

Dad was right.

Steven went about three feet into the air, did a single flip-flop and landed with a loud grunt on his stomach, right on Zoopy's broad back.

He wrapped his arms around the dog's neck and whispered in his ear, "Okay, Zoopy, if you like me as much as I think you do it's time for you to save my neck."

Zoopy seemed to answer, *"Ah-oof!"*

Steven sat up on Zoopy's back and, using all his strength, reached over and grabbed Russell's shirt and snatched his friend up behind him.

Steven leaned down to the dog's ear and said, "All right, big boy, let's do this!"

Letting loose three more gigantic *"Ah-oof!"*s, Zoopy turned around and ran down the alley right at Agents Five and Six.

Agent Five screamed, "Mommy!" and put his hands over his face.

Agent Six stared at the black dog and the two boys charging at him and fainted.

Steven wondered which one was going to be more embarrassed later on.

Zoopy got about three feet from where Agent Five stood, and jumped. Steven, Russell and the dog sailed high over the agent's head and landed ten feet on the other side of him.

The only thing blocking their way now was the brown SECRET GOVERNMENT CAR. But in one great bound Zoopy flew completely over the car.

They landed on Liberty Street only twelve blocks away from the Downtown Bank. All they had to do was turn right on Seventh Avenue, then go straight. In another twelve blocks Steven and Russell and Zoopy were going to be quadrillionaires!

ELEVEN

It Doesn't Hurt
Till You Get to the Bottom

STEVEN YELLED, "YAHOO! ZOOPY, YOU'RE the best dog ever! And since dogs are man's best friend I guess that means you're my best friend ever!"

Russell said, "Hey, what about me?"

Steven said, "The three of us are best friends ever."

He looked back at Russell, whose arms were wrapped tight around his waist.

"We did it! You're gonna be able to buy a whole storeful of mountain bikes!"

"I told you, Bucko, no problem, mon. Everything's irie!"

Behind them the six government agents had all piled into the two cars and came screeching out onto Liberty Street. Steven looked over his shoulder and saw that Agent Four was leaning out the window of the car with his little satellite dish pointed right at them.

Zoopy was fast but he was no match for these cars. Steven knew their only chance to get away now would be to run through backyards until they got downtown.

They came to Seventh Street and, just like he was reading Steven's mind, Zoopy turned right. The two cars that were trailing them screamed around the corner. The second car made the turn too sharply and slid into a tree. The three agents inside jumped out shaking their fists and screaming at Zoopy.

Steven and Russell couldn't help themselves—they both started laughing. But maybe they should've been paying closer attention because the first car had pulled right up beside them and Agent Four reached out the window and grabbed at Russell's leg.

"Hey!" Russell said. "That's no fair, stop!"

Agent Four finally got his hand around Russ's ankle and yelled, "Aha! I've got you, you little thief!"

"Uh-oh," Steven thought, "what to do? If I could only make Zoopy stop running along the street and turn into someone's yard they wouldn't be able to follow us."

Steven closed his eyes and concentrated as hard as he could, trying to send a message to Zoopy.

"Turn right! Turn right! Turn right!" he said over and over in his head.

Russell yelled, "Bucko! Help me!"

Agent Four leaned farther out of the speeding car's window and got his other hand around Russell's foot. Just when the agent got ready to snatch Russell into the car it seemed like all Steven's concentrating paid off and Zoopy turned sharply to the right.

Zoopy's turn pulled the government guy right out of the car's window. He let go of Russ's ankle, landed in the grass next to the curb and said, "Ooof!"

"Hey, Bucko, these secret agents play kind of rough, don't they?"

Steven laughed. "Don't worry, Russ, we've lost them, and besides, I've learned the way to control Zoopy, I can get him to go wherever I want him to!"

They tore through people's backyards, jumping over fences and small garages and barbecue grills, headed straight toward downtown and tons of money!

Steven yelled back to Russell, "All I've got to do is think 'right' and Zoopy turns right. All I've got to do is think 'left' and Zoopy turns left. All I've got to do is think 'straight' and Zoopy goes straight. The only thing I haven't figured out how to do is to get him to slow down, but that's okay, that just means we'll get down to the credit union faster than ever!"

"Have you ever had so much fun in your life, Russell?"

Russell had to think for a second. He wasn't sure if this was quite as much fun as the time he'd eaten twenty-five hot dogs in ten minutes. He said, "I think this *might* be the most fun ever because I probably won't have to throw up when we're done."

They jumped over a very high fence and for a second Steven caught a glimpse of the most famous landmark in Flint.

"Look, Russ! It's the weatherball! Just about seven blocks away!"

The weatherball was on top of Flint's tallest building, which happened to be the Downtown Bank. The ball was shining bright red.

"All we got to do is head toward it and we'll be safe."

Steven was so happy that he started singing the Weatherball Song. Every kid in Flint knew the song. Each morning at school they'd say the Pledge of Allegiance, then sing the Weatherball Song. It was sort of like Flint's national anthem.

"When the weatherball is red . . . ," Steven sang.

"Higher temperatures ahead . . . ," Russell answered.

"When the weatherball is blue . . ."

"Lower temperatures are due. . . ."

The weatherball was six blocks away.

Steven sang, "Yellow light in Weatherball . . ."

Russell replied, "Means there'll be no change at all."

The weatherball was five blocks away.

"When colors blink in agitation . . ."

"Means there'll be precipitation."

The weatherball was four blocks away.

Russell said, "Uh-oh."

"What's wrong, Russ?" Steven asked. "Only three and a half blocks to mountain bike city! Three and a half blocks until I can buy everything in the Back-of-the-Comic-Book catalog!"

"Uh-oh! Look!" Russell said, pointing just ahead of them.

"The only thing I can see is a quadrillion dollars getting closer and closer!"

"There." Russell's finger pointed at a tiny black and orange spot about forty feet above and in front of them.

Steven laughed. "Don't be such a chicken. That's just a monarch butterfly, it can't hurt you."

"I know, Bucko," Russell patiently said. "I hate to be the one to burp your bubble, but that's what Zoopy's been running after, you haven't been telling him where to go. Sqwoo-ros, mail trucks, mos-kwee-toes and butterflies are a few of his favorite things to chase."

Steven said, "Well, we've only got two more blocks to—"

Up above, the butterfly suddenly flitted right, and Zoopy jerked after him so quickly that Russell and Steven nearly fell off his back.

The weatherball was only three blocks away but now they were going in the wrong direction!

The butterfly must've caught a tailwind because it was going twice as fast as it had been before. Zoopy picked up his speed to follow.

The dog got going so fast that Steven had to lean down and squeeze his neck to keep from being blown off.

Zoopy reached Dort Highway, one of Flint's busiest streets, and turned right, heading out of town right behind the butterfly.

"Russell," Steven screamed, "we've got to get off, he's going to take us too far away. These monarch butterflies migrate all the way to Mexico. What if Zoopy doesn't stop until we get there? We gotta let go!"

Russell was squeezing Steven's waist and wasn't about to let go.

Zoopy ran south on Dort Highway just like he belonged there. People in cars looked over and pointed at the strange sight of a giant dog and two ridiculous-looking boys galloping down the road. In every car they passed people's eyes got big and their mouths looked like they were all saying "Whoa!"

"Russ," Steven yelled, "unless that butterfly slows down it's too dangerous to let go!"

"You don't have to tell me that, Bucko," Russell yelled back, "we're on Zoopy's back all the way to Mexico, *amigo!*"

Suddenly Zoopy turned off Dort Highway and began tearing through backyards.

As he bounded over someone's garage little droplets of water began dripping on Steven's face.

"Hmmm," Steven thought, "that's strange, the weatherball wasn't flashing for rain and there aren't any clouds in the sky."

Russell said, "Double uh-oh!"

"What now, Russ?" Steven asked.

"It really is time to get off him *now*, Bucko."

"Are you kidding, Russell? We're going way too fast and he's jumping way too high!"

Almost as if to prove Steven's point Zoopy jumped over a twenty-foot tree. A squirrel in the tree saw the dog coming, dropped his nuts and fainted right on his branch.

The drops of water started coming harder and harder.

"Sorry, Bucko, it's even more dangerous to stay on now."

"How come?"

"Zoopy's sprunged a leak. When you ride him it's fun for a while but pretty soon he gets too hot and you know what happens when a dog gets too hot."

Of course Steven knew how dogs cooled themselves, he was the second-smartest kid at Clark Elementary, after all. "They open their mouths and—"

Whap!

The left side of Steven's face felt like it had been smacked by a wet rolled-up newspaper.

Whap!

The right side of his face got the same treatment.

Zoopy's tongue was whipping back and forth, almost killing Steven!

He closed his eyes and tried to lean even closer to the dog's neck but there was no escaping the slippery, slobbery, sloppy pink tongue.

Whap! Left.

Whap! Right.

"Russell, what to do?"

"Well, Bucko, I'm outta here, looks like I'm not going to Mexico after all. If you want to stop him from running all you got to do is put your . . ."

All Steven could hear was Whap! Left. Whap! Right.

Steven felt Russell's arms let go of his waist and Russell was gone.

Whap! Left.

Whap! Right.

Between the smacks of Zoopy's tongue Steven looked

back and saw Russell tumbling in the dirt of someone's backyard. Russell jumped up and waved at Steven just as the giant tongue came back and resmacked the left side of his face.

Whap! Left.

Whap! Right.

He closed his eyes and held on as tight as he could but the pounding was becoming too much. It would be almost impossible to do any good reasoning with something as yucky as Zoopy's tongue hitting you in the face but Steven knew that the best thing he could do was not let go.

Whap! Left.

Whap! Right.

"What to do? What to do? How would a good detective get out of this mess?"

Whap! Left.

Whap! Right.

Steven's shirt was soaking wet with dog slob and his hair looked like he'd just taken a shower with some kind of foamy thick bubbly shampoo.

He thought, "Before Russ fell off he said there's a way to make Zoopy stop running, what could it be?"

Whap! Left.

Whap! Right.

Zoopy jumped again and this time it felt like the two of them were flying high enough to touch the moon!

The dog's tongue was pounding Steven so hard that it seemed like his ears had gone bad, it sounded like somebody was running the water in the bathtub full blast.

"Wait a minute," Steven thought, "if Zoopy really is only following that doggone monarch butterfly then all I have to do to get him to stop is make sure he can't see it!"

Steven opened his eyes, unwrapped his arms from around the giant dog's neck and put his hands over Zoopy's eyes.

Zoopy came sliding to a stop.

He felt Zoopy's heart pounding through his back like a bagful of rowdy boys.

He and Zoopy both fought to catch their breath.

Steven waited for the sound of crashing water to leave his ears. He shook his head a couple of times, but the noise was still there.

"Oh, man," he thought, "some of Zoopy's slob must've gotten into my ear canal and is sloshing around in there."

Finally his breathing slowed to normal and he looked to his left.

He closed his eyes right away, not believing what he'd just seen.

"Not possible," he said aloud.

He opened his eyes again.

When he looked to the right he saw an enormous lake. When he looked to his left he saw a two-hundred-and-fifty-foot drop into the churning, chugging waters of the Flint River!

Zoopy had run to the top of the Kearsley Reservoir and had finally stopped right in the middle of the top of the dam!

Still keeping his shaking hands over Zoopy's eyes,

Steven slid off the dog's back. The top of the dam was very wide so there wasn't any real danger that they'd fall off as long as they stayed in the middle. He could see that their main problem was going to be getting back to shore because each end of the dam was covered by a forty-foot barbed-wire fence.

He looked high and low, left and right to make sure there were no butterflies flitting around so he felt safe enough to take his hands away from Zoopy's eyes.

"Well, Zoopy," he said, "how are you at swimming? Looks like the only way outta here is to jump in the lake and swim to shore."

Zoopy wasn't in the mood for swimming or walking or anything but lying down on his side and trying to get a little rest. He'd missed his first four afternoon naps and jumping over twenty-foot fences and thirty-foot garages was enough to get the biggest, strongest dog in the world tired so Zoopy flopped onto his side for a quick snooze.

Steven understood, he was pretty tired too. "Great idea, boy, we'll wait here until you're good and ready."

He plopped himself down next to Zoopy and rested his head on the dog's chest.

Steven looked to his right again and said, "You know what? That old saying is right, money really is the roof of all evil. That doggone quadrillion-dollar bill has been nothing but trouble."

He dug down into his pants pocket and took out Mr. Chickee's funny money. He stood up and walked to the side of the dam that faced the lake.

He thought back to his yellow legal pad, where he'd written, "If money starts making me act weird or do crazy things, burn it, bury it, get rid of it, give it away."

Looking at the picture of the hardest-working man in show business, he said, "Mr. Brown, I hope you don't take this personal, I know it's not real easy being Soul Brother Number One in the twenty-first century and I know being the Godfather of Soul isn't as important as it used to be, but still, I just don't want you around."

Steven folded the quadrillion-dollar bill into a paper airplane and looked out over the lake.

He shouted, "Whoever wants this is welcome to it!"

He threw the quadrillion-dollar airplane into the air. The bill floated thirty feet across the lake, then caught a gust of wind and began to rise.

Up, up, up, it went.

It turned and started floating right back to where Steven and Zoopy were.

"Good riddance!" he shouted when the bill blew high over his head.

Steven didn't know why but he felt like a million bucks as he watched the bill lazily drift the two hundred and fifty feet toward the Flint River.

Zoopy scrambled to his feet, let out another gigantic *"Ah-oof!"* and jumped over the dam trying to catch what he thought was a strange new green butterfly.

"No!" Steven screamed, and grabbed Zoopy's tail! Just like that he was sailing over the dam right after his best friend in the world.

The last thing he noticed before he passed out was Zoopy's nasty, yucky pink tongue plucking the quadrillion-dollar airplane out of the sky, then disappearing into the dog's mouth. The last thing Steven said before he passed out was "Hmmm, falling two hundred and fifty feet isn't as bad as I thought it would be, this doesn't hurt one tiny bit."

A newspaper said that the splash the two made when they hit the river could be seen all the way at the top of the Downtown Bank in Flint.

The headline read "YOWCH!"

TWELVE

Being Famous Is No Good
if One of Your Best Friends Is Dea . . .
(Oops!) Gone!

STEVEN WAS TRYING TO FIGURE out if it was legal to be grounded by your parents until you were forty-five years old. But legal or not, that was exactly how long Dad had told him his punishment was going to last for doing something as irresponsible as riding a dog down Dort Highway without a helmet, then falling off the top of the Kearsley Dam.

"I wonder if that means if I get married and have kids that they'll have to be grounded too? I wonder if you can inherit getting grounded like you can inherit money? But maybe by then I'll be able to afford a good lawyer and he can get me off. If Mom and Dad let me out to get a job."

He couldn't remember anything that happened on the first day he'd been home. He'd been way too nervous and tired to do any scientific or investigative thinking. One thing he did know, falling two hundred and fifty feet over a dam made you kind of scared and jumpy about everything, even if you were at home in your bed.

Mom had checked out a book at the library called *Dealing with the Involuntarily Airborne Child* and told Steven that what he was feeling was quite normal and common. She said he was probably still in shock.

All he could do on the second day was think about Zoopy and cry. Even though he was almost ten years old Steven cried and cried. He cried so hard and so much that the tears defied gravity and instead of rolling down his cheeks they shot sideways out of his eyes right into his ears.

Mom and Dad came into his room and held him and patted his head and said not-very-helpful adult things like "It's all right, son" and "Don't worry, Steven, you'll feel better" and "Zoopy really loved you and I'm sure he's up in doggie heaven right now looking down on you and smiling."

Wow! That was about the dumbest thing Dad had ever said. Smiling in doggie heaven? Of course Zoopy was in doggie heaven but who'd ever heard of a smiling dog? Zoopy was probably looking down at Steven right now and drooling. But it did make Steven feel a little better to think that somehow Zoopy was still around, even if his friend was floating around as far from Flint as heaven.

"Maybe," Steven thought, "I'd stop feeling so bad if I got rid of all the things that remind me of Zoopy."

He dug under his bed and found the nine rolls of toilet

paper that he kept to soak up Zoopy's drool and threw them in the trash.

Mom and Dad found them and worried but didn't say anything. Mom spent a lot of time at the library looking for any books that might explain what your troublesome, involuntarily airborne, special child might do with nine rolls of toilet paper, but the librarians came up empty.

Next Steven looked in his top-secret safe and found the experimental shoe that Zoopy had always enjoyed chewing. It went right into the trash too. Steven remembered how the first time Zoopy had climbed in his bedroom window the huge puppy had picked up the shoe and waddled over to the foot of the bed and collapsed and chewed happily until he fell asleep.

Then Steven went to the kitchen and got paper towels and window cleaner. He stood outside his bedroom window right in the middle of Mom's geraniums and scrubbed at all the nose prints Zoopy had left on the glass. Whenever one of Zoopy's adventures took him to the Carter house he would let Steven know he wanted in by smushing his nose on the window and letting out a couple of "Ah-oof!"s.

"Yuck," Steven thought as he wiped at all the smudges, "not only was Zoopy's mouth all leaky, his nose was a pretty good runner too!"

He even got his mini-rake and scratched all Zoopy's footprints out of Mom's geranium bed.

So that was it. There was nothing more to ever remind him of Zoopy.

Nothing but those crazy dreams.

Four times on the third night after they'd gone over the dam Steven had dreamed that Zoopy was at his window. He dreamed that he could hear Zoopy's nose smushing against the glass and even dreamed he heard a couple of "*Ah-oof!*"s.

But by the time Steven jerked awake and ran to the window there was always nothing.

The next morning there was a tap-tap-tap at Steven's bedroom window.

It was Russell.

Steven automatically started feeling better. He hadn't seen his friend since he and Zoopy had fallen over the dam. He went over to let Russell in. As he pushed open the window he noticed a couple of Zoopy's nose prints on the glass that he'd missed when he'd cleaned the glass earlier.

Even though Russell was there Steven felt sad all over again.

"Heya, Bucko."

"Heya, Russ."

Russell had a bunch of newspapers in his hand.

"So, Bucko, you still in trouble?"

"Yup, until I'm forty-five years old. How about you?"

"Mummy and Daddy said they're going to ship me to Jamaica so Granny Forde could straighten me out and so I could be away from bad influenzas like you."

What could Steven say? He *had* been a bad influence on Russ. Any kid in the world who had just a little bit of sense would know that riding a large, silly dog down a busy highway *was* a pretty terrible idea.

"So when do you have to leave?"

"They changed their mind. I got a bunch of crying in on them and now they say that I can stay but that I can't be a Flint Future Detective anymore. I'ma wait a little longer and get some more crying in and they'll probably change their mind about that too. So don't kick me out of the club yet, okay?"

Steven didn't want to break the news to Russell but without Zoopy there probably wouldn't even be a Flint Future Detectives Club anymore.

"Sure, Russ, don't worry about it."

Russell said, "Whew!" and pretended he was wiping sweat off his forehead.

"How come you're carrying all those newspapers around, Russell?"

"Oh, I almost forgot. I wanted to see if you could sign these for me."

"Sign them for what?"

" 'Cause you're real famous now and maybe I can go on the Internet and sell them on WePay and I can still get one of those mountain bikes." Russell handed Steven the stack of newspapers.

The first paper was the one that had the headline "YOWCH!"

Russ reached in his pocket and pulled out a page of notebook paper and a crayon and handed them to Steven.

"This is a Special Signing Crayon, Bucko, and the note-book paper tells you what you gotta write on all the news-papers when you sign them."

Russell had written with the special purple crayon:

> I, Steven Daemon Carter, rilly do swair that I
> no Russell B. Woods and that I am the sam
> boy that fel over a dam and that I did not di
> and that the feds wer rilly chazen me and my
> best frend Russell B. Woods I swair two that
> Russell B Woods nevir cam to my house and
> axed me to sing this. Russell B. Woods prablee
> fount this on his fron poerch wher Steven put
> it late at nite. I did not talk to Russell B.
> Woods after I fel over a dam. Not efen one
> time. I rilly swair it.
> Singed bye Steven Daemon Carter.

Russell said, "I hope you don't care that I said you were my best friend."

"Why would I care, Russ, it's true."

Russell said, "Whew!" again.

"But this is going to take me a long time to do, Russell. Maybe you'd better leave me the papers."

"No problem, mon. Can I come back tomorrow and visit you some more?"

"Sure."

"How about later on today?"

"Sure."

"How about in half a hour?"

"Sure, Russell, but I won't have all the signing done."

"That's all right, Bucko, you don't have to sign those if you don't want to, I just wanted to see if you were mad 'cause me and Zoopy got you in so much trouble."

"I'm not mad, Russ, just sad."

"That's why we gotta visit each other even if we get in trouble for it, right?"

Steven said, "Right, but not too much 'cause I don't want you to get grounded too."

"Okay, Bucko, see you later, I gotta go feed my new dog anyway."

"*What?*"

"I forgot to tell you, Mummy and Daddy got me another dog. Hold on, I'll show him to you."

Russell reached in his pocket and pulled out the smallest dog Steven had ever seen. The dog was shaking and looking nervous.

"Who can blame it?" Steven thought. "It looks like a fly could snatch it up and take it away."

He asked Russell, "What kind of dog is that?"

"Daddy says it's a perfect dog. It doesn't eat much, it hasn't barked yet and it never drools."

"What's its name?"

"Mummy says it looks like a rat so we call him Rodney Rodent. You probably think that's a stupid name, huh?"

"Uh-uh, I think that's a perfect name."

Russell smiled and said, "Great! I'll sneak back later, Bucko. See ya."

Steven knew the responsible, mature thing would have been to tell Russell that since his parents didn't want them seeing each other they shouldn't sneak around. He figured he'd have that much responsibility and maturity in five or six years. Right now he just needed to see his friend.

When Russell walked away Steven looked down to see how much damage Russ's size twelves had done to Mom's geraniums. He hadn't crushed too many of the red and white flowers.

"Good," Steven thought, "I'm not going to have to do too much raking. But, doggone it, there are some more of Zoopy's footprints that I must've missed, I'd better get rid of them."

Steven used his mini-rake to scratch Russell and Zoopy out of Mom's flowerbed. Then he took some paper towel and wiped a few more old nose prints off the glass. Being careful not to leave any footprints of his own in the dirt, he climbed back into his bedroom.

He picked up Russell's Special Signing Crayon and the stack of newspapers and flopped down on his bed to begin.

"Boy," he thought, "I knew I was going to be famous one day and would have to sign autographs for people but I always thought it would be for solving some great mystery, not for falling over a dam."

As Steven read the different newspapers he couldn't believe how famous he'd become. For the past four days there had been articles about him in the Flint newspaper, both Detroit papers, *America Today* and the *National Inquisition*.

Some of the articles made him feel special, like the one

that said "Special Miracle Boy Survives Plunge of Terror." Some of them made him sad, like the one that said "Was the Dog That Fell Over the Dam and Disappeared Really an Alien Who Was Called Back to His Spaceship?" Some of the articles made him feel like a little goofball, like the one that said "Little Goofball Falls Over Dam." Some of them made him feel confused, like the one that said "Dolt Defies Death with Daring Dam Dive!"

"What's a dolt?" he wondered.

"Oh, well, maybe I'll look it up in that dictionary, it couldn't say anything to make me feel any worse anyway."

Steven went and checked Great-great-grampa Carter's old word book.

He couldn't help himself, he looked on the copyright page first.

He read, "Maybe I've been a little harsh with you before, I commiserate (*[ke-MI-ze-rat']* v. *To feel or express sorrow or sympathy for, empathize with, pity*) with you and hope you'll be feeling much better very soon."

Steven felt his eyes start to get watery.

He closed the cover and said, "Really? You really know how bad I feel?"

He opened the book again and read, "PSYCH! (*[sīk] n. slang. Derisive term indicating one is the butt of a joke. Often said in utter contempt.*) Of course I don't know how bad you feel, and what's more I don't care. Quit feeling sorry for yourself and get on with your life, you dolt."

Steven remembered that the word *dolt* was the reason he'd come to the dictionary in the first place.

He turned to the *D* section and looked up *dolt*.

He wished he hadn't. He read, *"Dolt (dolt) n. Blockhead. Dullard."*

But then, right as he watched, the letters on the page started separating and marching around! When they finally stopped Steven saw *"Dolt (dolt) n."* Then instead of a definition there was a picture of him!

"Man," he thought, "this dictionary isn't giving up any love at all!"

He went back to his room to start signing the papers for Russell.

He wondered if he should correct Russell's spelling and punctuation and syntax but decided these words were Russell's and it just wouldn't be fair to change them. Besides, only somebody real strange would even think about changing the words that another person had written.

After signing fifteen newspapers Steven decided to take a break. The Special Signing Crayon was about an inch shorter than when he'd started and there were two deep, deep grooves on the tips of his thumb and his pointing finger. He thought if he signed one more paper the bones in his fingertips would start poking through.

He began reading other articles in the papers to take his mind off Zoopy and what had happened. That meant he didn't look at anything that started with the words *Dam* or *Fall* or *Dog* or *What an Idiot*. The most interesting thing was in the Flint paper, an article that any Flint Future Detective would want to investigate.

POLICE CHECK TRAVELING CIRCUSES
TO SEE IF ANY ARE MISSING A BEAR

The bear that has been sighted for the past two days in a local south-side neighborhood is thought to have escaped from a traveling circus. Flint police are on the lookout for the creature estimated to weigh five hundred pounds and considered to be very dangerous and very hungry. The bear was first spotted by Mr. Jamal Thompson, 12, who stated, "It stole my whole box of Twinkies and nearly scared me to death!" Flint Police Chief Henry Younger said at an afternoon press conference, "Anyone spotting the bear is advised to run like crazy and don't call me, I'll call you."

"Hmm," Steven thought while scratching his chin just like an investigator, "this looks like something the Flint Future Detectives should really look into! A bear that big shouldn't be too hard to track down. Tomorrow I'm going to call Russell, and me and him and Zoop . . ." Then he remembered.

The tears headed right for his ears again. The only good thing was that between the raking and signing and thinking and hard crying he was so tired that he fell fast asleep.

THIRTEEN

Chow Down, Big Hound, Chow Down!

THAT NIGHT THE ZOOPY DREAM came back again, but now it was weirder than ever! Steven dreamed he heard the nose smushes and a couple of *"Ah-oof!"*s around midnight again, but this time when he ran to the window and opened it there stood Zoopy!

Steven didn't even care when the dog jumped through the window and gave him a couple of big, sloppy kisses, it was so good to see his friend again! Zoopy wagged his tail so much and so hard that all the papers and books on Steven's desk flew around the room. (Not that anyone would've noticed.) Even the clothes that Steven had carefully wadded and thrown on the floor went sailing.

After he gave his friend a big hug Steven stood back and looked at Zoopy. He knew he was dreaming because Zoopy looked kind of skinny, like he hadn't eaten in a while.

"Wait here a minute, Zoopy," Steven said, "I'll get you something to eat."

Steven went to the kitchen and opened the refrigerator.

Since this was a dream he thought it would be okay to really load his old friend down with food. He took the turkey the Carters had had for dinner that night and the dressing and what was left of the mashed potatoes. He took the big hunk of cheese and the can of whipped cream and the carton of milk. He took a dozen eggs and a carton of orange juice and a bottle of ketchup.

The he went to the cupboard and took the Crisped-Out Crunchos he ate every morning along with the two loaves of bread and the giant jar of peanut butter.

"Hmm," Steven thought, "Zoopy looked like he was really hungry. I'd better get him some dessert."

He went back to the fridge and took out two half gallons of ice cream. He also picked up the cake Mom had ordered for him with the frosting that said "We Love Our Talented, Gifted, Very Special Son."

Then he looked in the back of the highest cupboard and grabbed the four-year-old box of Wheaties where Dad had hidden his Triple Chocolate Double Butter Extra Sugared Candy Delights. (The commercial on television said, "They're so good, the tooth decay is worth it!") Dad thought no one in the world would ever look inside an old box of Wheaties so if he bought anything superspecial he'd hide it from Steven in the box. He should've known, though, that a Flint Future Detective would investigate anything as suspicious as a four-year-old box of Wheaties.

Steven loaded everything into three paper grocery sacks and headed back to his room. Zoopy sat up as soon as he smelled the food in the bags and closed his mouth with a loud *clop!*

"First, Zoopy," Steven said, "I'd better make sure this stuff is fresh before I give it to you."

Steven tilted his head back and sprayed a mouthful of whipped cream down his throat.

"Yup, fresh as morning dew!"

Zoopy tilted his head back and Steven squirted the rest of the can of whipped cream down the hungry dog's throat.

"I know this turkey leg is fresh, we had it for dinner just tonight."

He stuck the giant drumstick out to Zoopy and the dog swallowed the whole thing with one mighty *"Ga-loomp!"*

"Wow!" Steven said. "Let's see if you can do that with the rest of the turkey." He took a ruler and stuck the whole leftover turkey on it and held it toward Zoopy.

"Ga-loomp!" No more turkey.

"What's turkey without mashed potatoes and dressing?" Steven asked. He reached in the container and pulled out a handful of mashed potatoes and threw them down Zoopy's throat, the same with the dressing. Ten handfuls and some serious chops-licking later both containers were empty.

Next the big brick of cheese disappeared into Zoopy. "Easy come, easy go," Steven laughed. "Man, it's a good thing this is a dream, Zoopy, you're eating all the Carters' meals for the next four days!"

The eggs, shells and all, the orange juice, the milk, the Crisped-Out Crunchos, the whole bottle of ketchup and the two loaves of bread disappeared in a hurricane of "*Ga-loomp!*"s.

The cake and ice cream were gone like they'd been at a birthday party for thirty-five hungry eight-year-olds. Steven pulled Dad's Triple Chocolate Double Butter Extra Sugared Candy Delights out of the Wheaties box.

He said, "Since this is just a dream it's okay if you eat these things, Zoopy. Besides, the way you're swallowing everything whole there's no chance in the world they'll get on your teeth and give you cavities!"

The little sugar bomb candies vanished into Zoopy in less than a second.

Steven laughed and got ready to throw the Wheaties box in the wastebasket.

"Why be wasteful?" Steven thought. "It's just a dream," and he dumped the stale four-year-old Wheaties down Zoopy's throat next.

The giant dog made a sour face and with a mighty "*Patooh*" spit all the Wheaties out. They sprayed around the room and all over Steven like flakes of wet brown snow.

Steven laughed and wiped the mess off his face. He said, "I guess you weren't *that* hungry, huh?"

Zoopy stood anxiously waiting for more, the melting ice cream and cake frosting spilling out in a drooly mess.

"Not full yet? How about some peanut butter?"

Steven had forgotten to bring a spoon but he remembered that he'd sneaked a bowl of chocolate pudding and a big tablespoon into his bedroom a couple of weeks before.

"Now where did I leave that?" he asked himself. "Maybe under the bed."

He pulled his covers up, moved a couple of things around under his bed—all right, he moved a couple of hundred things around under his bed—and sure enough, there was the bowl. The only problem was that the spoon was stuck to the bowl so hard that it would take five days of soaking to get them apart.

Being a very flexible thinker, Steven knew what to do. He carefully put the bowl back under his bed, dug his hand into the king-sized jar of peanut butter and pulled out a fistful.

"I hope you don't mind, Zoopy, Mom says I'm a little too hyper so she buys sugar-free, salt-free, flavor-free peanut butter. If they were telling the truth they wouldn't call this junk peanut butter, they'd call it peanut ashes!"

Zoopy didn't mind at all. He licked the peanut butter from Steven's fingers like it was honey.

"Hmmm," Steven said, "is it that good?" Zoopy had missed a couple of hunks of the peanut butter around Steven's fingernails.

"Since this is a dream, I guess I can do it in the name of private investigation," Steven said, and licked the last bits of peanut butter off his fingers.

"Wow!" he thought. "Not bad! The sweetness from the ice cream and cake in Zoopy's slob and the natural dog-mouth saltiness make this stuff taste pretty darn good! Almost like real peanut butter, just a little tangier."

He dug out another fistful and he and Zoopy raced to see who could finish first.

That was enough. Zoopy's eyes rolled around in his head, his stomach grumbled and he let out a long, warm, disgusting burp.

Steven couldn't help himself, he laughed as hard as he could. There's something about being nine years old that makes you think a burp is the funniest thing in the world.

"That's strange." Steven sniffed the air. "That burp doesn't smell like all the junk you just ate at all, boy, it smells more like . . ." Steven figured, "This is a dream, so why not?" He pulled open Zoopy's mouth, stuck his whole head inside and took a deep breath.

"Yup, it isn't anything like a turkey dinner, it smells more like Twinkies! This is the strangest dream that could ever be."

Zoopy waddled over to the window, let out a slightly less disgusting burp, then jumped down into Mom's geraniums and waddled away.

"See you in my dreams tomorrow, Zoopy. Midnight, okay?"

Steven walked over, closed the window and crawled back into his bed.

"I guess if the only way Zoopy visits me is in my dreams then that's all right, at least I get to see him."

With that thought Steven fell asleep.

The next morning a terrible scream woke Steven.

Dad yelled, "Not the Triple Chocolate Double Butter

131

Extra Sugared Candy Delights! That's just not possible! How did he know where they were? How could one kid eat a week's worth of food?"

A few seconds later there was a light knock at Steven's door.

Mom.

"Steven? Are you up, sweetheart? May I come in?"

"Yes, Mom."

Mom looked at Steven and gave a little gasp.

"How are you today, son?"

"Pretty good."

"Steven," Mom said, "I'm going to get right to the point. You know we think you are such a special, delightful child, right?"

"Right."

"And you know if something is bothering you, you can tell us, right?"

"Right."

"And if we weren't feeding you enough you'd let us know, wouldn't you?"

"Wow," Steven thought, "this is even stranger than most of the things Mom comes up with. I sure hope I don't have to put up with this for another forty-four years, eleven months, three weeks and three days."

He answered, "Yes, Mom."

Mom said, "Good. We just want to let you know if you need more to eat all you have to do is tell us, okay? You would never have to sneak around to get food. Never."

"Yes, Mom."

Mom walked to the door. "Never, ever, never." She looked at the mess, thought about saying something but decided not to. She shook her head and closed the door.

Steven couldn't wait to see what book Mom had checked out from the library this time.

After Mom left, he went to the bathroom to brush his teeth. Well, he *thought* about brushing them anyway. As soon as he looked in the mirror he could understand part of the reason Mom was acting stranger than usual.

There was a big yucky ring of dried peanut butter around his mouth, and the front of his pajama shirt was covered with sticky globs of melted ice cream and cake. There was even half of a Triple Chocolate Double Butter Extra Sugared Candy Delight stuck in his hair. There was also a light coating of half-chewed Wheaties all over everything.

"Man," Steven thought, "I must've walked in my sleep and done all those crazy things I dreamed about! But if I did that and ate all that food how come I don't have a bellyache? Something is very strange here."

Steven started to clean himself up but before he could even wet a washcloth there was a knock at his window.

It was Russell.

Steven did a double take. Standing next to Russell was the smartest kid at Clark Elementary, Richelle Cyrus-Herndon!

He rubbed his eyes, wondering if this was another dream. But there she stood, with her hand on her hip and a look on her face like she wasn't believing what she was seeing.

Russell said, "Heya, Bucko."

"Heya, Russ."

"Uh, guess who this is, Bucko."

"How many guesses do I get?"

"How 'bout three?"

Steven said, "Richelle Cyrus-Herndon, Richelle Cyrus-Herndon, Richelle Cyrus-Herndon."

Russell was amazed. "Boy, Bucko! See what I told you, Richelle? He really is the second-smartest kid at Clark Elementary School!"

Richelle said, "I'm *so* impressed!"

Russell said, "I know you can't have a real club with only two people in it, Bucko, so I asked Richelle if she wanted to be a Flint Future Detective since you-know-who is up in doggie heaven."

Richelle started tapping her left foot and said, "I told him I wasn't making any promises but I would think about it."

Steven got ready to say "Don't bother," but Russell reached in through the window and snatched the half a piece of Triple Chocolate Double Butter Extra Sugared Candy Delight from Steven's hair.

"What's this?"

Steven said, "Yowch!"

Russell turned the chocolate over a couple of times, sniffed it, opened his mouth, looked at Richelle and said, "This smells and looks pretty good, even with all that brown junk on top of it, but Mummy says I gotta quit eating anything with hair on it that's not my own."

With a sad look Russell licked the chocolate so it was sticky and put it back in Steven's hair.

Steven pulled it out and popped it in his mouth. After all, Russell's mom was pretty smart and this *was* his hair. Besides, Triple Chocolate Double Butter Extra Sugared Candy Delights were so good, it didn't really matter whose hair was on them! Or how much of a coating of stale Wheaties they had on them. And he was hoping this would gross Richelle out so much that she wouldn't want to join the club.

But she didn't squirm or make any kind of sour face. All she did was stand there with her hand on her hip and her left foot tapping and now she rolled her eyes back in her head.

"So, Bucko," Russell asked, "you excited about the meeting?"

"Russell, I know tomorrow is Saturday, but I don't think the Flint Future Detectives are going to have any meetings for a while."

"That's kinda sad, Bucko, but that's not the meeting I meant."

"Then what did you mean?"

"The meeting with the fed guys."

"Huh?" Steven knew he'd been banned from saying "huh" too, but Russell didn't care about things like that.

"Yeah, your mom and dad and my mummy and daddy and you and me and some lady who's the boss in Washington are going to meet today and straighten this whole mess out."

"What?"

"Maybe your mom told you and you forgot about it. Maybe Mummy was right. She said the last thing in the world you needed was to fall over a dam and get your brain more scrambled than it already is."

"I think I'd've remembered that. So we're all supposed to meet today?"

"Yup, the day after yesterday and the day before tomorrow."

"Where?"

"At Agent Fondoo's building."

There was a soft knock at Steven's door.

Russell whispered, "See you at the meeting! Come on, Richelle, Mummy said Steven's parents are skating close to the edge and I don't wanna do anything to send them over.

"Oh, yeah, Bucko, if anybody asks you, you didn't see me here." And Russell and Richelle ran off.

Steven started to close the window but stopped. "How can I keep missing Zoopy's nose prints on this glass? I swear I got 'em all off."

The knock came again.

"Steven, sweetheart?"

"Yes, Mom?"

"Are you up to talking a little bit?"

"Yes, Mom."

Mom and Dad came into the bedroom.

Mom asked, "How are you feeling, son?"

"Fine."

"How's the little bump on your head?"

"Not bad."

"And the scrape on your leg?"

"I forgot all about it."

"Good, good! It's so amazing that you are able to still feel fine after all you've been through!"

Dad's tone wasn't so friendly and supportive. "And how's your stomach?" he asked.

Mom elbowed him in the side.

"My stomach's fine, Dad."

Dad said, "I'll bet it is. I'll also bet that sweet tooth of yours has really been acting up lately."

This time Mom elbowed Dad so hard he said, "Ooomph!" and grabbed his ribs.

"Steven," Mom said, "you, your father and I and the Woodses have been invited downtown today for a meeting with some people about that strange piece of money that Othello Chickee gave you. Do you think you feel up to that?"

Steven had to think. Why would the feds want to meet with his and Russ's families? This could be some kind of trick to get them all together to send them off to jail.

Mom knew something was bothering Steven. "We really believe there's nothing to worry about, son. Agent Fondoo said he had something he wanted to give you. He also said someone from Washington would like to meet you."

That must be Madam Director!

"Well . . . ," Steven said.

"Good!" Mom said. "We'll leave in about an hour!"

Dad said, "Yeah, it's probably going to take you that long to scrape all that peanut butter off your—"

Mom grabbed Dad's ear and pulled him out of Steven's room.

"Hmmm," Steven thought, "maybe I'm about to finally solve the mystery of Mr. Chickee's funny money! But Dad's right, first I'd better get some of this peanut butter off my face. For some reason adults look at you kind of funny if you've got a ring of dried-up food around your mouth."

FOURTEEN

I'm Pleeztameechew 'Cause Everyt'ing's Irie!

WHEN THE CARTER FAMILY GOT to Agent Fondoo's office the Woodses were already sitting in the waiting room. All the adults looked at each other in a funny way. It seemed that Mrs. Woods still thought there was something a little too unusual about the Carters and their very different son. They barely nodded to each other. But Russell and Steven were another story altogether.

"Heya, Bucko!" Russell said, and ran over to give his best friend a hug.

"Heya, Russ!"

"It sure is nice to see you for the very first time since you fell over the da . . . oops!" Russell clapped his hand over his mouth and looked at his parents to see if he was in trouble. He'd forgotten that he wasn't supposed to mention what his mother called "the nonsense situation that strange boy got himself into."

"It's nice to see you again too."

Russell and Steven laughed at each other.

The door to the office opened and Agent Fondoo, still smiling his Crisco smile, said, "Well, well, well, I see we're all here, why don't you come in."

Agent Fondoo shook all the grown-ups' hands and gave Russell a dirty look, then gave Steven a double dirty look.

When Steven walked into the office Agent Fondoo introduced everybody to a very tall, very serious-looking woman.

"Mr. and Mrs. Carter and Mr. and Mrs. Woods, please meet Madam Director. Madam Director, this young man is Russell, and this other one is the little boy who fell over the da . . . oops!" Agent Fondoo clapped his hand over his mouth and looked at Madam Director to see if he was in trouble. He'd forgotten he wasn't supposed to mention what she had called "the ridiculous situation you and that strange little boy got into."

Russell said, "Hi," and the adults shook hands and made sounds of greeting.

Steven must have been feeling better. He started looking at the situation in an investigative way. "Hmm," he thought, "the way adults meet is just like the way dogs do when they see another dog for the first time. The big difference is instead of wagging their tails and sniffing each other, adults show their teeth and nod their heads. Look at the way Mr.

Woods and Dad both said the same thing to Madam Director, and look at the way she says the same thing back to them, what kind of sense does 'Pleased to meet you' make? I'll bet you anything that they aren't pleased at all to meet each other. And how come they say it like it was one word, 'pleeztameechew?' How come Dad hasn't had me looking that up in Great-great-grampa Carter's mean old dictionary? Seems to me like sniffing makes a whole lot more sense, even if it might get kind of embarrassing depending on who you were sniffing. And what's with all this—"

"Steven!"

Uh-oh!

"Yes, Dad," Steven said.

"Agent Fondoo introduced you to Madam Director."

"Steven," Madam Director repeated, "I've heard so much about you, I'm really pleeztameechew."

Steven couldn't believe it. He didn't really want to but he smiled, his mouth came open and "Pleeztameechew" fell out.

"Oh, no!" Steven thought. "This is like that famous experiment where those mean scientists were teasing dogs in Russia by ringing bells, then giving them hamburgers to see if they'd slob." As soon as he thought about slobbing dogs he thought about Zoopy. Steven didn't feel like a scientist at all, he felt like a sad little kid who was this close to crying.

"So," Mom said before Steven got a chance to get the tears going across his face sideways, "what exactly is the purpose of this meeting, Madam Director?"

The woman from Washington pointed at Agent Fondoo's desk. "What do you good American citizens see when you look there?"

"A desk," Russell's father said.

"A very messy desk," Russell's mother added.

"A very messy desk with a bunch of chewed-up pencils on it," Steven's dad said.

"A very messy desk with a bunch of chewed-up pencils on it along with several other obvious signs that life isn't going exactly as someone had hoped," Mom said.

Madam Director said, "Agreed. Boys, what do you see?"

Russell told her, "I see a empty box of Triple Chocolate Double Butter Extra Sugared Candy Delights!"

Steven thought before he answered, then said, "I see a desk with no chair behind it."

"Excellent reply, young man!" Madam Director shouted. "And where do you suppose that chair is?"

Steven had noticed the chair when he first walked into the office. "It's in the corner there."

"Most observant," Madam Director said. "And why do you suppose that chair is in the corner?"

Russell said, "Someone's about to get a time-out!"

"Bingo!" the woman from Washington said. "And who do we suppose that someone is?"

Every eye turned to Agent Fondoo.

"Correct," Madam Director said. "And why do we suppose Agent Fondoo is getting a time-out?"

"He didn't do his homework?" Russell said.

"Worse than that."

"He wasted taxpayers' dollars?" Mr. Woods said.

"Oh, that's nothing, it's much worse than that."

"He failed to file his income tax for the past ten years?" Mrs. Woods asked.

Agent Fondoo said, "Hey! It's only been eight . . . oops."

"Worse than that. Let's see if Agent Fondoo might know. Fondoo?"

Agent Fondoo seemed sad. "It's because I recklessly endangered the life of an innocent young pain in the ne—"

"Fondoo!"

"—an innocent young man because I had agents chase him until he fell over a da . . . oops!"

"Is that all?" Madam Director asked. "Seems to me there might be something more."

"I also caused a quadrillion-dollar bill to be lost or destroyed under a dam."

Madam Director said, "And . . ."

Fondoo hung his head. "And I'm real sorry that I did."

"And to whom are you directing that apology?"

Fondoo looked like he was sucking a lemon. "To Steven Daemon Carter."

"Then don't you think you should look at him when you say that?"

Agent Fondoo looked at Steven and said, "Sorry."

He didn't mean to, but Steven said, "That's okay."

"Man," Steven thought, "saying 'That's okay' is like saying 'Pleeztameechew,' it comes out without you even—"

Madam Director said, "Go on, Agent, finish what we talked about."

Agent Fondoo walked over to a second door in his office. The letters there said BRAD, DEUS EX MACHINA.

Steven thought, "Hmm, I'm going to have to look that up in Great-great-grampa Carter's dictionary."

Fondoo said, "Brad?"

A young man came in. "Yes, sir?"

Agent Fondoo said, "Everyone, this is Brad. Brad, this is everyone."

Brad said, "Pleeztameechew."

Steven's dad said, "Pleeztameechew."

Steven's mom said, "Pleeztameechew."

Russell's mom said, "Pleeztameechew."

Russell's dad said, "Pleeztameechew."

Steven said, "Pleeztameechew."

Russell said, "Hi."

"Brad, could you please bring in the first item?"

When Brad walked back into the other room Agent Fondoo said, "Sorry, Russell, if you were scared by the agents I sent to chase you. I know this can't possibly make up for your loss and suffering but I hope you'll take this as a sign of how sorry I am."

Brad came into the room wheeling a brand-new XR-P 1284 mountain bike, bright red with orange flames painted on the side!

"Wow!" Russell said. "Thank you very much! Can I keep it, Mummy?"

"Well . . . ," Mrs. Woods said.

"Thanks a bunch!" Russell said, and sat on his new bike making motorcycle sounds.

"Mr. and Mrs. Woods," Agent Fondoo said, "sorry if I caused you to worry about your son. As a token of my remorse please accept these."

Agent Fondoo handed an envelope to Russell's dad.

Russell's dad opened it and read what was inside. "Round-trip tickets to Jamaica for three, first class! Wow! Can we keep them, honey?"

"Well . . . ," Mrs. Woods said.

"Great!" Mr. Woods said.

"And Mr. and Mrs. Carter," Fondoo said, "sorry for putting your son in such terrible danger. Please accept these."

He handed Steven's dad a square package. Was Dad ever surprised when he opened it!

"It can't be, it's Billy Stewart's rarest white-label album! *Billy Stewart Teaches Old Standards, New Tricks!* With the . . ." Mr. Carter started choking up. ". . . with the extended version of 'Summertime'!"

A single tear left his eye and ran right back toward his ear.

Steven's mom opened her envelope. A huge smile crossed her face.

"A two-thousand-dollar gift certificate to Flint's last independent bookstore, the 'Bout 2 B Bust! The store with the largest selection of childrearing books in North America!"

Madam Director said, "Fondoo, aren't you forgetting someone?"

Agent Fondoo gave Steven another double dirty look, then looked away as quickly as he could. He didn't know why, but he had a feeling that this weird kid had something

145

to do with his mouth moving closer to his nose. All his years of secret agent training had taught him that if you had a bad feeling about someone you should trust it.

It was like the time he'd been captured on the Island of Boom-Cha—

Madam Director shouted, "Fondoo!"

"Oh! Steven, sorry I made a bunch of feds chase you until you fell over a da . . . oops! You know what I mean."

Steven clenched his teeth so "That's okay" couldn't jump out of his mouth.

"And . . . ," Madam Director said.

"And I know how good an investigator you're going to be so to show how sorry I am I bought this for you. Brad?"

The other door opened again and Brad brought in a briefcase.

Steven couldn't believe his eyes! When he opened the briefcase there was a brand-new XR-P 1284 laptop computer, bright red with orange flames painted on the top!

Agent Fondoo said, "It comes with a load of scientific software. It has worldwide wireless connectivity."

"Man!" Steven said, and booted the computer up.

As soon as it came on, a box popped up and Steven read:

Young Mr. Carter, I knew you'd pass the test! I'll be back soon and we can discuss what happens next while we're shopping for groceries. I'm craving a Vernor's, see you then! P.S. Keep this under your hat!

Mr. Chickee!

Steven closed his new computer and did his best not to let anyone know he'd seen something very mysterious. It only halfway worked, though. His ears started flapping back and forth.

Madam Director said, "Go on, Agent Fondoo."

"We've also loaded it with the latest technology that is designed to be used only by scientific geniuses and top-notch investigators . . ."

"Finish the sentence, Fondoo."

Agent Fondoo said, ". . . It's loaded with the latest technology that is designed to be used only by scientific geniuses and top-notch investigators . . ." He mumbled something no one could understand.

Madam Director shouted, "Fondoo!"

He looked quickly at Steven and said, ". . . top-notch investigators *like you!*"

Steven said, "Wow! Thank you very much! Can I keep it, Mom?"

Mrs. Carter said, "Well . . ."

Steven said, "Great!"

Madam Director said, "And the other thing, Agent Fondoo?"

Fondoo said, "Well, Steven, thanks to you, ever since the incident with the quadrillion-dollar bill I've been given several new responsibilities. My title has been changed from Secret Agent to Secret Agent Slash Animal Control Officer. My first job under this new title was to investigate the rash of bear sightings that have taken place on the south side of Flint these past few weeks. And to make a long story longer, Brad?"

The other door opened again. This time Brad tugged a long leash and every jaw in the office dropped.

Every Woods and every Carter yelled, "Zoopy!"

Zoopy charged right at Steven and Russell and gave both of them the sloppiest hellos he could come up with.

The boys didn't care. They laughed at their dripping faces and each other.

Mr. Woods said, "Uh-oh, Russell, have you forgotten about Rodney Rodent? We really can't have two dogs, you know."

Mrs. Woods added, "Yes, and as unpleasant an animal as Rodney Rodent is, we did make a commitment to keep him, so I guess Zoopy is going to have to find another home."

Mr. Woods said, "That's right, I've really become attached to that little dog. Looks like Zoopy's got to hit the road. Unless . . ." Russell's dad looked at Steven's parents.

"Unless nothing," Mr. Carter said.

Steven said, "Dad? Please? He wouldn't be any trouble. I'd clean up after him. I'd watch him."

"Steven," Mr. Carter said, "we'd love to take Zoopy, but we don't have anything to carry him around in. Our car is way too small."

Mrs. Woods yelled, "The van! Give them the van! And the food! We've got two barrels of his food left! Give it to them!"

Mr. Woods said, "No problem, mon, did I forget to tell you? The van belongs to Zoopy! Take him and you get his van! Not to mention a two-week supply of dog food!"

Mr. Carter said, "That's very kind of you, but—"

Steven's mom said, "I read in *Coping with the Moping* that a pet is wonderful therapy for a child who has been through what Steven's been through."

Steven's dad said, "Gerbils! Now, there's a great pet! Or goldfish!"

Steven said, "Can we keep him, Mom? That way Russ can come visit him anytime he wants to."

Steven's mom said, "Well . . ."

Steven yelled, "Yahoo!"

Russell yelled, "Wow!"

Mrs. Woods yelled, "What a relief!"

Mr. Woods yelled, "Thank you, Jesus!"

Zoopy barked, "*Ah-oof!*"

Dad openly sobbed. And guess where the tears went after they left his eyes.

Madam Director said, "Wonderful, nearly everyone is happy! Brad, could you bring in those GPO five-four-ones, please?"

Brad came in and handed some pamphlets to the woman from Washington. She gave each of the adults one. They showed a picture of an exhausted judge sitting at his bench with a pile of papers around him. The caption on the pamphlet said "Why It's Patriotic Not to Sue."

Madam Director said, "I must be getting back to

Washington. If any of you have any problems please feel free to get in touch with me."

She turned to Agent Fondoo and said, "Well?"

Agent Fondoo pouted and flopped himself in the chair in the corner.

Madam Director shook everybody's hand and left.

Russell's mom said, "The keys! Quick, give them the keys!"

Russell's dad said, "Right!" and handed Mr. Carter the keys to the van. "It's parked right on the street, don't worry about us, it looks like a beautiful day for a walk, it looks like a beautiful day all the way around! No worries, mon, every-t'ing's irie!"

Steven thought, "It sure is! What could be better? Agent Fondoo let Mom and Dad know that it wasn't my fault I fell over a dam, Zoopy is alive and fine and going to be living with us, and the Flint Future Detectives are back together! And we even have a real computer! The only problem is I know that doggone Richelle Cyrus-Herndon is going to try to take over being president from me.

"Man! We're really going to have to work hard too, there are a lot of mysteries going on right here right now!

"First, why was Zoopy running around on the south side all this week? Second, how did Agent Fondoo know exactly what each one of us really wanted? Third, how in the world is Great-great-grampa Carter's dictionary sending me those messages? Fourth, what did that message from Mr. Chickee on my new laptop mean? And fifth, how is it possible that

those tears are coming out of Dad's eyes and running sideways across his face right into his ears?"

Steven turned to Russell and Zoopy and whispered, "As
soon as we get home we've got a whole ton of investigative
thinking to do!"

About the Author

CHRISTOPHER PAUL CURTIS is the bestselling author of *Bud, Not Buddy*, winner of the Newbery Medal and the Coretta Scott King Author Award, among many other honors. His first novel, *The Watsons Go to Birmingham—1963*, was also singled out for many awards, among them a Newbery Honor and a Coretta Scott King Honor. His most recent book, *Bucking the Sarge*, won the Golden Kite Award from the Society of Children's Book Writers and Illustrators. Christopher Paul Curtis grew up in Flint, Michigan. After high school, he began working on the assembly line at Fisher Body Flint Plant No. 1 while attending the Flint branch of the University of Michigan, where he began writing essays and fiction. He is now a full-time writer. Christopher Paul Curtis and his wife, Kay, have two children and live in Windsor, Ontario, Canada.